Bezaliel's DESTINY
A Paranormal Romance
A 'Spirit' Mate Love Story - Book #6

© EJ Brock – March 2012

D1522920

ISBN-13 978-1470146412
ISBN-10 147014641X

Book cover photo byGMME

Bezaliel's DESTINY

Dedication

This book is dedicated to the memory of my many loved ones, who already reside in Paradise.

Fred, Jodi, SnowAnna, Hezekiah, Amanda, Lara, Donnell, James, Larry, Luther, Robert, Reba, Lillian, Aurellia (Baby Rose), and Justin.

I'll see you at the Estate...

Bezaliel's DESTINY

Acknowledgements

Thanks to Emma Brock, Freddie Leavy and Anita Miller for your continued support.
Thank God for increasing my territory.

Bezaliel's DESTINY

A 'SPIRIT' MATE SERIES

Brock's REDEMPTION –Book #1
Ramiel's SYMPHONY – Book #2
Denel's LILY – Book #3
Chazaqiel's HOPE– Book #4
Batariel's ROBYN #5
Bezaliel's DESTINY – Book #6
Arakiel's FAITH #7
WEDDINGS & BIRTHS #8
BARAQIEL'S DAWN #9
HENRY'S PIA #10
THE BROTHAS - #11
SEPARATE VACATIONS #12
YOMIEL #13
ADAM - #14
THE PROMISE #15

Bezaliel's DESTINY

Bezaliel's
DESTINY
(A Spirit Mate Love Story)
(Book 6)

A PARANORMAL ROMANCE

Bezaliel's DESTINY

PROLOGUE

A week had passed since the Watchers rescued mob kingpin, Sal, and his gay, nephew-bodyguard, Geno, from their so-called friends. Sal's son, Antonio, had put a hit out on him and Geno for testifying against him in the murder of his wife.

Batman's mate, Robyn, had witnessed Antonio murder his wife, in cold blood, and had spanked his ass for doing it.

Initially, Sal had wanted Robyn eliminated so she could not testify against his son. But, after experiencing the wrath of Batman, Sal had a change of heart and testified against his son, himself.

Knowing his, ruthless, son would retaliate, Sal and Geno became Robyn's protectors against Antonio and the rogue members of Sal's organization. Their act of valor forged a more-than-comfortable alliance between them and the Watchers.

But, in a well-organized sneak attack, Sal was shot in the stomach and left for dead in his home. Geno was captured and beaten, for information on Batman's mate, Robyn's, whereabouts. But, Geno refused to give them any information, because Robyn was an innocent woman.

Sal, badly, wounded and desperate to find Geno, had called out to Brock for help. The Watchers had been more than willing to remove any threat to Robyn and their new friends, Geno and Sal.

After the Watchers eliminated the threat and rescued Geno and Sal, Ali volunteered to escort them to Geno's house; because Sal's was no longer safe.

Ali had lifted both men in his arms and teleported to the front door of Geno's house. He hadn't wanted to teleport inside the house, and scare the hell out of Geno's life partner.

He'd knocked on the door, with his mind.

A beautiful woman opened the door...and he'd dropped both men! Ali and the woman stood there staring at each other. There was no doubt in his mind who she was or whose she was.

It was at Geno's house that Ali had,

surprisingly, found his 'spirit' mate. "Destiny!" he whispered.

"My E-du-di told me you would find me, Ali." Destiny's heart was racing, fighting to get out of her chest. He was as handsome as she'd seen. Tall, dark and hers!

Both of them forgot about the wounded men on the ground.

"What are you doing *here*?" Ali asked her.

"This is my brother, Nantan's, home." She still didn't notice the men on the ground.

~

Ali had, immediately, sent a shout out to the team that he'd found Destiny and that she was *his* 'spirit' mate. He'd also informed them that Geno's life partner was Destiny's brother.

The team was excited for him, including Arak and Baraqiel. They felt it wouldn't be long before they found their own 'spirit' mates.

~

At Ali's request, Brock told the Walker family the good news that Destiny was Ali's mate. He also told everyone, except Ditto, that Destiny's brother, Nantan, was Geno's significant other. After the way they'd teased Ditto about Geno being romantically interested in him, Brock wanted to tell him in private.

Everyone understood that to mean that, through Nantan, Geno and Sal were now a part of their ever growing family. The family was okay with Geno and Nantan being gay and assured Brock they were not homophobic. The nephews claimed to be friends with Ditto's best friend, who was also gay. Everyone secretly laughed at the fact that Geno would now be a part of their family. After the way he'd goo-goo eyed Ditto and JR, this was going to be interesting.

Kwanita was elated, plus she was glad her cousin was safe. She looked forward to her cousin living with them at the estate. She was also relieved to finally know where Nantan was. His parents had turned their backs on him once they found out he was gay. He'd disappeared fifteen years earlier and no one knew if he was dead or alive.

SnowAnna had wanted to go and get Nantan. To let him know he was loved. She was angry with E-du-di, because she was sure he'd known, all along, where Nantan was. And even though she was the *'mother'* of all secret keepers, she didn't like secrets being kept from her.

Jodi, Lara and Amanda had also been pleased, especially Lara. Not so much for Destiny, as for Ali. Ali was her husband's best friend. He spent a lot of time with them and she knew how lonely he was. He'd tease her saying, *'Lara, I hope my 'spirit' mate ain't as mean as you are, girl!'* But she'd come right back at him, *"If only you could be so lucky. Ya' heard.'* He'd squeak, with laughter.

Once he found out she was pregnant, after he finished laughing at her, he'd made her a vow. *'You are not a 'spirit' mate, but you don't need to be. I will stand with James in protecting you and this little one you are carrying'.* That had made her cry. Then he handed her a towel and made her laugh by saying, *'With all the money we have, we still can't afford to buy enough tissues for you hormonal women. Gee whiz, wipe your nose, girl!'* Yeah, she adored Ali and was happy for him.

The, non-related, 'spirit' mates on the Walker side didn't know Destiny as well as they knew Kwanita, but they were looking forward to getting to know her. She would be part of their sisterhood.

~

Now, Brock was sitting in his suite with his

favorite nephew, Ditto. It wasn't because Ditto was Cinda's son that endeared Brock to him, because Henry was her son, too. It was the fact that the boy was outgoing, had a good sense of humor, danced to the beat of his own drum and was open minded. He'd told Brock that his best friend, since junior high school, was gay. Well, Brock was about to see, just how good his sense of humor was, as well as his open-mindedness. Brock wanted to laugh at the irony.

"What's up, Unc?" Ditto asked him.

"You know that Destiny is Ali's 'spirit' mate."

"Yeah. That's tight. She's a good looking woman. We've been trying to get in contact with her. She does all of our legwork for the building permits."

"Listen man, I've teased you about Geno and you've been good natured about it. But, you know he's not interested in you…right?"

Ditto thought Brock had just changed the subject. "What does that have to do with Ali and Destiny?"

There was no way to sugar coat this, so Brock just let it rip. "Destiny's brother, Nantan, is Geno's life partner."

"Nantan! Quit playing, Unc!" Ditto burst out laughing. Then he noticed Brock wasn't smiling. This wasn't one of Brock's teases. His uncle was as serious as he was *'BLACK'*. He dropped his head and looked under-eyed at Brock. "Nantan's *partner!*"

He smacked his lips, shook his head and huffed. He couldn't believe that.

CHAPTER 1

Ali spent the week with Destiny, and her brother, nurturing Sal and Geno back to health. Although Sal had been shot, he *seemed* to be in good shape. But it was just his machismo that wouldn't allow anyone to know how much pain he was in. Ali had read his mind and knew he was struggling, both, physically and emotionally. Even though Antonio had betrayed him, he'd loved his son to the bitter end.

Antonio's funeral was today and Ali had volunteered to take Sal, cloaked with invisibility. When they arrived inside the church, they stood in the back and watched the procession of people walking around the casket. Ali and Sal agreed it was best if they were not in the crowd. For one reason, there would be a gap between the ones in front and ones behind them. And for another reason, Ali wanted room to move.

The church was packed with friends of

Antonio's and Sal's. Women were crying, leaning in the casket, claiming what a 'good' man Antonio was. Sal whispered to Ali, "It's a shame the way people lie, in the house of God, ain't it."

Ali almost laughed out loud. He put his finger up to his lips. "Shh"

Sal smiled, but Ali could see the turmoil in his eyes. He held Sal's arms as he escorted him down the aisle. They needed to view the body before the casket was closed. Sal stroked Antonio's face and then crumbled in Ali's arms and cried, "That's my *son*!"

Well, damn! Ali wasn't expecting that! He'd never gone to a funeral and didn't know people cried out loud, so he hadn't cloaked their voices. Some of the mobsters reached for their weapons and started perusing the crowd, trying to see where Sal was located.

There were two separate groups at the funeral. They were enemies of each other, and of Sal. Once word spread that his son had put out a hit on him he became everyone's target. If he couldn't control his own son, he couldn't control the organization. That was their creed, *'handle your business or we'll handle 'it'…and you'.* Both groups wanted Sal's territory and figured they'd attack, while he was down. There was no doubt, in Ali's mind, that Sal could not come back to this life. He wasn't even sure Sal wanted to.

Ali immediately teleported out, but he couldn't leave these innocent people in danger of getting shot by the two rivaling mobs. He gave all of the, gun toting, gangsters a mild gastro attack. The only thing they'd be fighting over now was the john.

~

The minute they returned to the house, Geno took possession of, a sobbing, Sal. "It's alright, Uncle," he said, hugging the man.

Salvador stiffened and wiped his eyes. "I am not your Uncle!"

"I know. We have told that lie for so long, I don't know if I can call you anything other than that."

"What lie?" Nantan asked.

"Geno is my *son*. Not my nephew."

Nantan looked at Geno and frowned. "Son?"

"Yes," Geno said, looking like he knew he

should've told Nantan the truth, years ago.

"Come on, Darlin', let's let them talk in private." Ali pulled his shades down, grabbed Destiny's hand and teleported to the park.

~

Ali and Destiny had been together for a week. They spent their days taking care of Sal and Geno and their nights dining and dancing. Destiny knew he was just as attracted to her, as she was to him, but he made no advances toward her. He'd tried, on more than one occasion, to return to Jodi's house but couldn't pull himself away from her. He slept on the couch…every night. And although Destiny tossed and turned in her room, and beat her pillow in frustration…Ali slept like a baby!

Now they were strolling through the park, holding hands. Every once in a while he'd stop, caress her cheek and kiss her. His full lips were rugged, but tender. And although the man kissed like he invented the art of it, she wanted more. But that was as far as he'd go. She was giving him all kinds of signals, that she was more than willing; but not once in the past week had he made a single advance toward her.

"Ali, why do you not try to seduce me?" Destiny finally asked. "Are you a virgin?"

He laughed and put his arms around her waist. "No, Darlin', I am not a virgin. Well, actually I guess I am, in a sense."

She'd always appreciated a big man, but he was the sexiest man she'd ever met. From the moment she'd opened the door at Nantan's house her once dormant libido leaped into overdrive. Everything about his physique had her body screaming for an introduction. His eyes were dark and alluring. The way he looked at her was a testament that she was not the only one yearning for their coupling. After years of being mocked for being plus sized, his massive arms made her feel dainty and petite. In addition, he was bowlegged. Now if that wasn't just the sexiest thing! No wonder her system was in shock. Who would've ever thought she'd end up with the man of her dreams and the answer to her prayers: tall, dark, handsome and bowlegged to boot! She could almost hear God whisper, *'I heard ya', Destiny'*.

"A virgin in a sense. What does that mean?" she asked and rubbed up against Ali.

He groaned, then grabbed her hand and walked over to a park bench. He first let her sit and then he sat down beside her. He put his arm around her shoulders and gazed across the park. "I have secured this park, every night, for the better part of one hundred years. I've witnessed the violence of man's inhumanity, against each other, under the veil of darkness. I've fought bitter battles, against demons, on these very ground." Then he looked down at her. "But, I've also seen couples in love, walking in this park, holding hands, laughing and enjoying each other's company." He pointed to a section concealed by tall hedges. "On moonlit nights they lay in the grass, over there, having late night picnics- sharing wine, feeding each other small bites of cheese and strawberries. I've seen them kissing, caressing and staring into each other's eyes; acting like the world around them was nothing more than an artist's canvas. I've vicariously felt their desires stir, with the anticipation of what was to come next. Their physical need, for each other, so strong, it was sometimes unbearable for me to witness. I promised myself that when I found my 'spirit' mate..." He kissed her hand "...you, Darlin', I'd romance you."

Destiny sighed and leaned back into his shoulder. She loved the way he sensuously described couples in love. His deep, African accent, was tantalizing her senses and stirring a desire within her that she'd never felt. She wanted what those couples had, too. She wanted to gaze in his, beautiful, dark eyes and see that same anticipated desire. "I've never been on a picnic," she admitted, and then confessed, "I've never been in love, before you."

"I've never been on a date." Ali smiled. "I want to wine and dine you; and do all the things I've seen humans do, to fall in love."

"But we are, already, in love," she protested.

He kissed her hand. "Yes, but we haven't been on a picnic. We haven't seen a movie together, Darlin'."

She laughed. "Don't tell me you want to take me on one of those scary movie dates. The ones that will make me hide my face in your chest."

"Now there's a thought." He smiled. "I want us to share it all. But right now, I am enjoying sitting here, in broad daylight, with you. This is my first time sitting in this park, just for the joy of it. I am happy to be enjoying it with you."

"You never take your shades off, until the sun goes down."

"I'll go blind if I do."

She didn't know that. She looked at him. "What?"

He kissed her fingers. "It has only been a few months that I've been able to walk in the daylight."

"I didn't know that, Ali."

"Your cousin, Kwanita, and her husband, Yomiel, developed these glasses so we Watchers, can enjoy the park during the day."

For him to have spent all those centuries never seeing daylight, made her want to cry. "You've always been in the dark?"

He smiled. "There is no darkness for us. Midnight, for us, is as bright as noon day."

"No darkness, at all? What about when you sleep."

"Well, yeah, there's that." He laughed.

~

They sat for a while, just enjoying the

moment.   Ali was experiencing a peace that surpassed his, analytical, understanding.   They sat watching other couples walking, holding hands and playing.   For the first time in his existence, he didn't feel like a voyeur.

He, now, understood what Brock meant when he'd said he no longer just existed.   This was living.   He was living!   He wasn't going to squander his time with her on the fundamental aspects of a relationship, like making love.   And although he had an urgent need, and desire, for her; they had the rest of their lives, for that.

He wanted to share all of creation with her: parks, beaches and movies.   He wanted them to share the exceptional, like visiting other countries; and the mundane, like folding clothes.   And although they wouldn't age, he wouldn't mind growing old with her.   He could see them sitting in their rocking chairs on the porch, finishing each other's sentences.

He kissed her hand again and whispered, "I've waited a long time for you, Darlin'."

~

She laid her head on his chest and listened to

his breathing. He was a beautiful man, with a beautiful heart. "I am glad that my brother and his lifestyle don't offend you, Ali. I've feared, for a year, that you would treat him like my parents, and sister, have."

"How do they treat him?"

"They don't. They have all disowned him. He is no longer welcome in their home or community. He hasn't seen them in over fifteen years. E-du-di and I are the only family that has accepted him. I spend my time between his house and E-du-di's."

"I am sorry to hear that. But I like your brother and Geno is a hoot."

Then he told her about Geno's perusal of his and Brock's bodies, and how he refers to Ditto as "sexy man."

She laughed. "He just talks a lot of smack; he has always been faithful to Nantan. They are both starved for acceptance."

Then it registered what he said. "Is that why you have not taken me to the estate? Does Ditto have a problem with my brother being gay?" She knew, and worked for, Ditto. She would be hurt if that was the reason.

"Not at all. There are too many of your family members there. I am selfish, Darlin'. I don't want to share you. I know once I take you there, your cousins will whisk you away from me."

She smiled. "So what does your team think about Nantan?"

"They haven't met him, but they really like Geno. We came to this very park that night, to rescue *him*. Ditto's best friend is gay, so he has no problems..." Then he laughed. "...Just so long as Geno doesn't come on to him."

"He'd never do that. He just likes to have fun."

"He told us some humans were mean to them, because they were different. Our mothers died bringing us into this world. They were robbed of the privilege of ever holding us. We've had very little interaction with humans and we had no idea that a mother could actually turn her back on her child." He shook his head. "We will be Nantan's and Geno's family; and Sal's too."

Her eyes watered. "Thank you for that. I love my brother, Ali."

He kissed the top of her head. "And I love you, Darlin'."

~

By the time they returned to the house Sal had changed clothes and was watching TV. "How are you feeling, Sal?" Ali asked and sat beside him.

"I'm better, thank you. May I ask you a question?"

"Sure."

"Who killed Antonio?"

Ali searched but couldn't find malice in his questioning. "Yomiel."

"Which one is he?"

"He's Brock's brother. The one we call 'Doc'."

"Oh, yes, now I remember. Is it possible for me to speak with him?"

Ali sent a shout out, *"Doc."*

"Yeah, Dawg, what's up?"

"I told Sal you were the one to kill Antonio. He would like to talk with you."

"Why?"

"Don't know. But he's cool. There's no malice in his request."

"Okay, because when I come, Kwanita will want to come see Destiny."

"No prob. Bring her."

"Will he come?" Sal asked.

"Yes, he wanted to be sure it was safe to bring his wife, Kwanita."

"Kwanita's coming?" Destiny and Nantan said, at the same time.

~

Before Ali could answer, Doc and Kwanita appeared in the room. Kwanita hit Ali. "Everyone at the estate is pissed at you, Ali!"

"Why?" he asked, innocently.

"You know why. Why won't you bring Destiny home?" She scowled at him. "Everybody wants to see her!"

Ali smiled. "Didn't I tell you, Darlin'? They will steal you from me."

"You are being selfish, Ali," Kwanita scolded him. "Aunt SnowAnna is really pissed. I'm surprised your ears aren't burning from the names she's calling you."

"Leave Ali alone and give me a hug, Nita," Destiny said, with open arms.

"Hey cuz." Kwanita hugged Destiny and rocked them both back and forth. Destiny was her favorite cousin. She was six years older than Kwanita, but she'd never treated her like she was a kid. "I'm so happy to see you."

Then she noticed Nantan, standing off to the side, nervously watching them. "Nantan! I didn't know you were living in Indiana, this close to me! Aunt SnowAnna can't wait to see you, either."

Nantan frowned. "She wants to see me?" He was so used to his family shunning him; he never tried to reach out to Kwanita or SnowAnna. A person could only take so much rejection.

Kwanita hugged him. "We are not like your parents, Honey. We love you just the way you are. We're your family, now, okay?"

Nantan hugged her so tight, she couldn't breathe. He'd been afraid she'd reject him and embarrass him in front of Geno and Sal. "Thank you, Nita. I needed that."

"I…can't…breathe." She laughed. When he eased up on his hold, she said, "Now introduce me to your partner."

Geno was on his best behavior. "Hello

girlfriend. Your man is hot!"

Doc shook his head and rolled his eyes. Kwanita, Destiny and Ali burst out laughing. "My man told me all about you." Then she hugged him.

Nantan had spent too many years isolated from him family. He was grateful for Destiny and E-du-di, but to now have Kwanita and Aunt Snow's support made him smile. "What about Lara, Jodi and Amanda, Kwanita?" They were his cousin's too. He still didn't want to subject himself or Geno to, unnecessary, discomfort.

"They are all waiting to see you, Honey. So is Uncle Hezekiah. Everyone is pissed at Ali, and I do mean pissed. It's not safe for you guys out here."

"Don't pay that woman no never mind. I can keep you all safe," Ali rebutted her. "She just wants to steal my woman!"

"Well, so what if you can, everybody wants her to come home…tonight!" Kwanita frowned.

"It ain't gonna happen. So get over it." Ali frowned back at her.

"Hey, stop arguing with my woman, Dawg! She is right." Doc frowned at him. "And you *know* she is!"

"You, and *your woman,* need to back off and let me handle my business!" Ali shot back at Doc. "I'll bring Destiny, when the timing is right. Not a minute sooner! Ya' Heard!"

Both Doc and Kwanita left it at that.

~

Doc turned around and greeted Sal. "How are you doing?"

"I've been better," Sal said, standing. "I understand you are the one who killed Antonio."

"Yes, sir."

Sal extended his hand. "Thank you for not marring his face. I understand your brother wasn't so gentle with the other guys."

Doc was glad he'd been right about not putting Antonio in the grinder. "I wanted to make it as easy on you as possible. I wasn't sure if you'd want to have a proper burial for him."

Sal nodded his head. This man had done him a great honor. "Do you have time to sit with me, for a while?"

"Yes."

~

While Doc and Sal talked, Kwanita got reacquainted with both her cousins. Geno was clowning Ali. From all appearances they looked like one big happy family.

"Geno, you know Arak is still waiting on you and Sal to teach him how to play poker," Ali informed him.

"Anytime. Anywhere," Geno said.

"Listen, fun and games aside, Kwanita is right; living at the estate would be safer. At the funeral today there were two additional mob factions there, looking to kill Sal. But there are some things that have to be worked out, first."

Geno knew the other mobs would come after his father. It wasn't that they had an allegiance to Antonio or Sonny, but that was the nature of their business. Kick the dog while he's down. He was his father's only protector now. If he could convince Sal, he'd hide him anywhere Ali offered. "Like what?" Geno asked.

"First of all, I need to know if you, and Sal, are finished with that life. I won't bring trouble to our doorstep and endanger my family."

"I am and I am sure my father is, too. We

can't just walk away, though. They'll be looking for Sal, trying to make their bones. They won't ever stop, Ali."

"You could walk away, if there was no way for them to find you."

"True that." Geno remembered how Salvador's men tried for months but couldn't find the woman who'd attacked Antonio.

"Second, I need to have you and Sal meet with Batman's woman and her family. We need to make sure the air is clear, if you get my drift."

"I'd love to see her. That woman can fight."

"Third, we have children living at the estate. We grownups have no problem with your lifestyle, but we don't want to confuse the children."

"So what are you saying?"

"Behave yourself and don't flirt with the guys, *man*!" Ali laughed.

Geno laughed. Then he got quiet. When he'd first met them, they'd told him they were Nephilim, angels. Warriors for humanity's soul. He didn't understand why they were so nice to him. He wasn't used to that.

"Is that a problem?" Ali asked.

"No, but I was thinking, humans cast us aside. Other than my father, my entire family disowned me. The same thing happened with Nantan and his family. Yet, you guys are *angels* and you welcome us with open arms. Why is that?"

"We were not sent here to judge humanity. Our commission is to keep humanity safe from the Fallen. We fight evil whenever and wherever it pops its ugly head up, like Sonny and Antonio. But none of you are evil, not in your hearts. Did you know your father never wanted to be a mobster? That he'd wanted to be a priest."

"Yes. That's why he was accepting of me, because he'd been denied his calling. He knows what it feels like for other people to make choices *for* you."

"Couldn't he have just said he wasn't interested?" Ali asked.

"Not in this business. The enemy would have taken him out; just to be sure he didn't change his mind, later."

"That's messed up, man," Ali said, feeling even sorrier for Sal.

"That is the life we were born into. You

don't just walk away from the Mob. We are stuck."

"Not anymore." Ali smiled.

CHAPTER 2

Batman and Brock arrived at Geno's house with Robyn, her parents and brother. Ali had invited them to come to the house for a private meeting. It was a good idea to let them work through whatever differences they might have. Luther and JR had mixed emotions, but they were willing to give it a try.

Ali told them not to pretend. If it was still a problem after they met, no one would force them to accept Sal and Geno. He'd make other provisions.

~

Brock insisted Ditto come along, too. He wanted to see how he interacted with Geno. If Geno made his favorite nephew uncomfortable, it would, also, be a 'no go'. He'd spoken to Chaz about putting a host of his guards around Geno and Sal, until they could find them a safe place to live.

Elijah had suggested the still vacant SOGA Bed and Breakfasts in New Jersey, as an alternative place for Geno and Sal to stay. They needed to do something with those buildings, anyway. He didn't want them and neither did Brock.

The team was hoping it worked, because they wanted to learn how to play poker. Ram wanted to play a game of pool with Geno. Besides they just plain, and simply, liked Geno and Sal.

~

The minute they arrived, Ditto saw Geno and attacked him. He smacked him upside his head and started choking him. "I ought to kick your, sorry, ass!"

Brock was about to stop Ditto, when he heard him say, "Since when is your, *damned,* name Geno!"

Geno was laughing the entire time Ditto was choking him. Then Ditto stopped choking him; and they hugged each other. "That's my real name, man. It's short for Eugene. Amongst my uncle's people, they call me Geno. It's the whole Italian thing. But my mother wasn't Italian and she named me after her father." He kept laughing.

"You didn't go by Geno in school!" Ditto frowned.

"The teacher wouldn't let me. They knew my

background." Geno kept laughing. "I had a ball with your friends, man. I knew it was you the minute I saw you from the roof of the courthouse. When you looked up, I almost waved at you. But I wasn't about to let those bastards, Bruno and Bonito, know I knew you. Although, I didn't know it was Robyn we were aiming at, until Brock let me see her kick Antonio's ass." He looked over at Robyn and laughed, again.

Robyn punched him. "I can't believe you were going to shoot me, Eugene!" She hadn't seen him since she was a little girl.

"We ought to kick his ass, anyway," JR said. "You pointed a gun at my sister, Eugene!"

Geno shook his head. "No, I didn't! I never saw her, Luther. I only saw *you* guys walking in the courtyard. I had no idea you were coming to court for Antonio's trial. I kept trying to distract those bastards, by pointing out you and Howard to them. None of them could stomach my being gay, although Vito and Vinny were more accepting. So I was picking on them the whole time; hoping to give Robyn a chance to get inside the courthouse. Even though I didn't know it was Robyn, at the time," Geno explained.

"You're still a jackass. I don't know why I put up with you," Ditto said, and popped him upside his head again.

Then he walked over and greeted Nantan. "How you doing, Cuz?" Ditto had known Nantan was related to his cousins, but had kept their friendship a secret, because Nantan's family had ostracized him. He didn't want his friend to suffer anymore rejection. People were too opinionated about things that didn't make a cat's scratch, worth of difference in their own lives. Being gay wasn't like having a contagious disease or anything. He was secure in his heterosexuality. He loved himself some women, one in particular. But he wasn't, in the least bit, ashamed to have Eugene and Nantan as his best friends. They both meant the world to him. He had his mother to thank for his open mindedness.

Nantan embraced Ditto. He was one of the few, straight friends, they associated with. They weren't related, but claimed each other as family. "Good to see ya', Cuz. Eugene's been messing with your head, again, I see." Nantan laughed.

"Man I told you, years ago, you should lock his sorry ass up and throw away the key, didn't I?" Ditto pointed at him. "That boy ain't ever gonna be right."

Nantan felt good. They hadn't ever had family around them, other than Sal and Destiny. Not even Antonio would come near them. They had lots of friends in the gay community, but he didn't want to be identified as *just* gay. He was more than his sexual persuasion and he wanted everyone to accept him, as such. He had a degree in Computer Science and was one of the most prolific game designers in the world. He'd even developed all the applications Howard and Henry used in their construction company; from invoicing and graphic designs, to payroll. "When did you figure out it was Eugene?" he asked, smiling.

"When my Uncle said, 'Geno' was *your* partner. At first I thought he was playing. Then when I saw the look on his face I knew that bastard, Eugene, had been jacking with me."

"Did you get your sugar?" Geno laughed, and threw him a kiss.

Ditto gave him his middle finger.

~

Everyone else, including Sal, was staring at and listening to them. They were getting the gist of it but they wanted answers, especially Brock. "Ditto, care to enlighten the rest of us?"

"I told y'all my best friend was gay. I just forgot to tell y'all he was mentally challenged; and a blight on my, no nonsense, reputation!"

"So, Geno is your best friend?" Ali asked.

Ditto frowned, as though it pained him to admit it. "Sad to say, but yeah."

Ali squeaked. "Man, Ditto, you sure know how to pick em." Destiny hit him, but he kept squeaking. Ali was relieved, though. If Luther and Earlie could deal with Sal and Geno, they'd be home free.

"Did you know he was Mafia?" Brock asked.

"No. He told me he was orphaned and lived with his uncle. I befriended him because my mother grew up an orphan, too. I felt sorry for his sorry, butt. He would never let me come to his house when we were growing up. He didn't want me to meet his uncle. He said the man was mean and abusive."

"Geno!" Sal yelled at him.

Ditto decided on a little payback. "Man, he said you were ugly, too."

"Geno!" Sal yelled, again, and then laughed. "Well, that part might be true."

"I didn't tell him you were ugly!" Geno said, and hit Ditto. Sal was, ruggedly, handsome in a Robert De Niro sort of way. Geno looked like him. "I did say you were mean. I had to tell him something. When Papa died you were thrust into this world of violence, even though it wasn't what you wanted. You dragged me into that world, because you had no choice. I don't blame you for that; but I wasn't about to let my, only, friend be caught up in it. I didn't want him to know you were a mob kingpin. Or come to visit and be caught in the middle of a bad situation," Geno said, and then looked at Brock. "Howard was the only friend I had in school. When we were in junior high school the boys, in gym, used to bully me, because I was gay. Howard always stood up and protected me. He was the only one who would sit with me at the lunch table. He taught me how to defend myself." Then he looked at Ditto. "You say you felt sorry for me..." He shook his head. "...but, in truth, you know you liked me."

Ditto smiled, because that was more than true. "Yeah, I liked you, Dawg." He finally noticed the bruises on Geno's face. "I didn't teach you how to get your fool head bashed in, like this, man," Ditto said. Everyone watched as he, involuntarily, balled his fist. "Who did this to you, Eugene?"

"They caught me off guard. Sal and I thought they were on our side and let our guards down," Geno explained. Then he told Ditto how it happened. "Your friends rescued me...and killed them."

Then Geno looked at Robyn. "If I had *known* it was you, or anyone in your family, I would have killed Antonio, while he slept..." Then he nodded his head towards Ditto. "...for my friend's sake."

Ditto nodded his head because he believed his friend. He had no doubt that Eugene would kill for him; even his own cousin. Ditto had protected him all throughout junior high school. He'd even gone to school sick, because he knew Eugene would be jumped, if he wasn't there. He hated bullies. His mother, Lucinda, had told him how lonely she'd been as an orphan. She'd told him the kids used to pick on her, just because she didn't have a family. He would never let anyone do that to Eugene.

He'd taught Eugene some of the moves James taught the family and helped him buff up. By the time they got to high school, Eugene was six-three, and a force to be reckoned with. They had remained best friends after all those years. And would remain so, until the day they died.

~

Brock recognized that protective nature in Ditto. Ditto, like all the Walker men, fought for the underdogs. He may not have had a right, but he was proud of his 'favorite' nephew. He was reading their thoughts: Geno, Nantan and Ditto were more than friends…the three of them were family. Yeah, he was unbelievably proud of Ditto!

~

Batman grabbed Robyn's hand. "Sal, you remember my wife, Robyn."

"Yes. These must be her parents?" Sal said, and extended his hand.

"That's right, I'm her father, Luther, this is her mother, Earlie, and her brother, JR."

"I am deeply sorry for my, misguided, attempt to harm you, young lady. I am even sorrier that you had to witness what my son did to his wife. I did not raise him to be abusive to women."

There was no mistaking the sincerity in his voice. It was apparent the man had had a change of heart. Luther and JR couldn't hold anything against the man. His son was dead and yet, he was still able to admit how brutal he was.

Robyn had been nervous about coming here. She didn't quite believe Batman when he'd said the man was okay. But looking at him now she could see he was hurting over the loss of his son. Yet, he didn't blame anyone, except maybe himself. "It's okay. I'm sorry he tried to kill you, too. I've changed my line of work. I won't be fighting, abusive, men anymore," she said, honestly.

"I know that's right!" Batman agreed.

"But girlfriend you're *fierce!*" Geno laughed.

Batman growled. "Not anymore, she's not, Geno!"

Robyn laughed. "You wait until my cousins find out you were going to shoot me. Those girls, and I, are going to kick your ass!"

Geno laughed. "I'm *scared* of you, girlfriend."

Brock nodded. He remembered when Hezekiah had used that phrase, on him, and hurt his feelings. It made sense to him, now. In the context that Geno was saying it, he was giving Robyn props for her fighting ability.

~

Sal looked at Luther and Earlie. They were a striking couple. They looked like they were high socialites, but down to earth. As masculine as he was, she was just as feminine. She didn't really look old enough to have children as old as Robyn and JR, but they looked like her. He looked like a man who could handle his business, with his bare hands; and yet be gentle to his family. He wanted these types of people in his and his son's lives. Decent, family, people. "My son was getting ready to put some steaks on the grill. Do you all have time to share a meal with us?"

"That would be nice, but who is your son?" Luther asked. Luther was trained to read a person, by their body language and voice. Even in the midst of Sal's grief, he could tell that this man was genuinely a nice person. How in the world did he get involved with the mob?

"Geno is not my nephew. He is my oldest son."

"Son!" Ditto said, frowning at Geno. "I ought to kick your ass, boy!"

Geno started laughing.

"Don't feel bad, Howard. I just found out the truth this morning," Nantan said.

Sal proceeded to tell them his life story. "I always wanted to be a Priest, but, because I was next in line to take over the business it wasn't possible. I met and fell, madly, in love with Geno's mother, Darlene. She was the most beautiful woman I'd ever met. She knew my family was mob, but didn't care. She loved me." He looked nostalgic, like he was still in love with her. "We got married when we were twenty."

"I thought Priests were not interested in sex," Robyn said, cutting him off.

"That's a common misconception. It's not that they don't have a desire for sexual companionship. It's that their desire to be of service is greater," Sal informed her.

"Color me a heathen then, because nothing is worth giving up sex!" Robyn frowned. Then she stroked Batman's cheek. "Especially good sex!"

"Robyn!" Both her parents said, at the same time.

Everyone else started laughing, including Sal. Batman blushed.

"Anyway, my wife, my father, my sister and her child, were killed in a car bomb. Geno was only three months old at the time. For his safety I decided to lie and say it was my child that had been killed and Geno was my nephew."

"Why?" Luther asked. "What difference would it have made, if he was your child?"

"They were not trying to kill my sister and her son. She wasn't a threat to the organization. She just happened to be at the wrong place, at the wrong time."

"If they'd known Geno was yours, they would have tried to kill a *baby*?" Luther asked.

Sal nodded his head. "With the death of my father the organization was weakened. If they could kill his only grandson, while the chips were down, they could take it over."

Luther shook his head. "So, I presume, they came after you."

"Yes, but they underestimated me! They thought I was too grief stricken to hold the gang together. They were wrong. I didn't give a damn about being a mob boss; but with the exception of Geno, they'd killed everyone I loved. The only thing I felt was vitriol and the need for retribution. I didn't seek, or want, help from the gang. This was personal. At first, I was able to pick them off, one by one. I killed them in their beds, in their cars, in the theatre, wherever. Pretty soon, everyone realized it was me doing all the killing. They came at me, in droves." He laughed hauntingly. "Foolish mistake. By the time the blood washed down the street drains, I'd solidified my place in the mob world, as one to be reckoned with. I'd earned the reputation of being ruthless, calculating and coldhearted. All true! The only person, in this world, I cared anything about..." He looked endearingly across the room. "...was my Geno." He and Geno smiled at each other. "Then I met Maria, she was a nice girl, but I didn't love her. We had Antonio. She soon tired of a loveless marriage and left me."

"You didn't try to stop her?" Robyn asked, remembering Antonio wouldn't let his wife leave him.

"No. I gave her a lump of cash and sent her on her way, with my best wishes." Then he bowed his head, as though in consternation. "But I would not let her take my son, Antonio. He never got over being abandoned by her. He never knew I wouldn't *let* her take him."

They were all thinking what a sad story. Tragedy had shaped this man's future. A future he did not want, but had embraced, nonetheless. They liked him.

~

"Brock, this is Destiny," Ali said, holding her hand. "Destiny, this is Jodi's husband, Brock."

Brock held her hand between both of his. Although she didn't look like SnowAnna, or Kwanita, she was very attractive. And a perfect match for Ali. He was happy for both of them. "It is good to meet you, Destiny. However, you and Ali have me at odds with my mother-in-law."

"Why?" Destiny asked.

"I tried to tell Ali," Kwanita said. "Didn't I?"

"Your Aunt is upset that you've been in town for a week, and she hasn't seen you. She wanted me to force you to come home but it wasn't my place to do so." Then he looked at Nantan; there was no need for a formal introduction. "She's furious to learn that you've been here for fifteen years and never once came to see her."

"I didn't know she'd want to see me," Nantan said. His father was SnowAnna's brother. He just assumed she felt the same way.

"Well now you know and you, both, need to get me out of the dog house. That cute, little woman is bossy!"

Brock turned to tell Sal and Geno that they were welcome to come to the estate when he stopped suddenly. Doc, Batman and Ali, all yelled, "Oh shit!"

Ali gabbed Destiny…Doc grabbed Kwanita…Batman grabbed Robyn, and vanished. Brock teleported everyone else out of the house… just as it blew up!

~

The women were screaming, when they

landed in the kitchen at the estate. Their eardrums felt like they'd burst. Ali's eyes were red. He was angrier than he'd ever been. "I thought you said nobody knew where you lived!" he shouted at Geno.

Geno was attending to his father. Sal was still healing from being shot. Brock had snatched them so fast he was afraid his father was hurt. "No one ever knew where I lived," Geno responded.

"Then how do you explain your house being blown to West Hell!" Ali shouted, again.

"I don't know. I'm telling you nobody knew, Ali!" he shouted back. God they could have all been killed. His hand started trembling.

Sal held Geno's hand still and stared him in the eye. "Antonio knew, son. Your brother knew."

"No! He can't be still trying to kill us! Not from the grave, Sal."

"It had to be him. Nobody else knew."

"Wait a minute. Are you trying to say Antonio reached from the grave and blew your damn house up?" Ditto asked.

"In a manner of speaking, yes, I am. If they hadn't found Geno and me together, they would have killed me. But then they would have had to kill Geno, because he would have picked them off, one by one. Without mercy! Antonio *had* to have told Sonny where Geno lived."

"That has to mean there are still some of your men out to get you, Sal," Brock said.

Sal palmed Geno's cheek. "He's right, Son." Then he looked at Brock. "We cannot stay here. We have caused your family enough grief. We will not put your family in anymore danger."

Ali felt bad for yelling at Geno. It wasn't his fault. It was that damned Antonio. "You *will* stay here, Sal; all of you. They can't get to you, here. I promise."

"Ali is right. Until we get to the bottom of this, you can't leave the grounds, for any reason," Brock informed them.

"We have caused your family much trouble, yet you continue to show compassion towards us," Sal said, humbly. "I am ashamed."

"Don't be concerned about the past, Sal. They are right, you, Geno and Nantan need to stay here," Luther said, and patted him on his back. He felt sorry for Sal. It had to be heartbreaking to have your son turn, so ruthlessly, on you. "We hold no grudges towards you or your son." Luther knew his saying it carried a lot more weight than Brock or Ali. After all it had been his daughter Sal had wanted to kill. But they, all, knew he was remorseful and wouldn't cause her any harm.

~

Everybody came into the kitchen to see what was going on. They'd heard the women screaming. "What happened?" Hezekiah asked.

It was obvious Destiny's ears were bothering her. SnowAnna walked up and pulled her out of Ali's arms. "What happened, Baby?"

When they told everybody what happened, SnowAnna yelled at Ali. "If you had brought my niece home this would not have happened to her!" Kwanita and Brock were right, she was pissed at Ali. "This is all your fault, Ali!"

"We had no way of knowing they knew where Geno lived. I would never put Destiny in danger," Ali defended his actions.

"He's right, Aunt Snow." Destiny was talking loud, because she couldn't hear. "This is not Ali's fault." She pulled away from Snow and went back to Ali's opened arms. "Leave him alone."

"Oh God, Wolf! Where is Nantan? Did you get him out? Where is he?" SnowAnna panicked. "Where is Nantan?"

Nantan has spent the last fifteen years blending into the background, trying not to be seen. He'd never been exposed to Geno's Mafia life, for his own safety. His family didn't want him. So, even at six feet three, he could be a shadow whenever needed. Tonight was no different. "I'm right here, Aunt Snow."

SnowAnna turned around and saw him standing up against the wall. "Nantan!" She opened her little arms and he walked in. She rose up and kissed his cheek. "My brother is a *fool!* If he and his wife don't want you, I do. You're home now. From now on, you are *my* son."

"Our son." Hezekiah embraced him. "You should have come straight to us, fifteen years ago, son. We would have stood by you. We would have taken you in." It vexed Hezekiah that Nantan had been on his own that young. He could kill his brother-in-law for doing that to his son. Twenty year olds think they are grown, but they are not. They are just over aged children. Addison was proof of that.

Jodi, Lara and Amanda, all, embraced Nantan. Jodi knew what it felt like when family walked away. She was teary eyed and couldn't speak. She just patted him on the back.

~

Henry and Mark noticed Geno at the same time. "What is Eugene doing here?" Henry asked.

Ditto smacked his lip. "Eugene is *Geno.*"

The Walker brothers, and their sons, started laughing. They all knew Eugene. They just didn't know 'Geno'.

"Man, you made Ditto have nightmares!" Mark informed him.

Hezekiah frowned at Ditto. "You knew all along that Nantan was in town and you didn't tell us?"

"I knew what his parents had done to him. I didn't want him to go through anymore rejection." That was the truth. They all knew that Eugene was his best friend, but he'd never, once, told them about Nantan.

"What kind of sense does that make, Ditto? We've never treated Eugene badly. What in the hell, would make you think we'd treat our 'own' any differently?" Howard scolded his son. He felt the same way Hezekiah did. Homeless at twenty was too young. The streets were cruel to throw away children. Degenerate lowlifes preyed on the children nobody wanted. He smacked Ditto upside his head, and not in a playful way, either. "The same kind of creeps that got a hold of Hope could have gotten Nantan, Ditto!" His voice cracked.

Ditto hadn't thought about that. He didn't answer, because he didn't know what to say to everyone staring at him. His family had accepted Eugene when he was fourteen years old and never once treated him like he was anything but part of the family. All he could do was rub his head...damn that hurt! He didn't appreciate being hit, by his father or anyone else. He was a grown ass man! But he didn't say that out loud. "I was just trying to protect my friend!"

"Wait a minute," Nantan said. "This is not Howard's fault. He was only a fifteen year old kid when I first arrived. He didn't know I was here until six years later, when I met Eugene. They were both grown and I was already settled by then." He didn't want these people to think he was a pedophile. "When Eugene introduced me to his best friend, we both recognized each other, right off. I made Howard promise not to tell, any of you, where I was." Nantan stood up for his friend.

"Why would you not want us to know?" Hezekiah asked.

Nantan closed his eyes and shook his head. "You did not see what my father did to me." He ran his hand from across his eyes, down his face to his neck. "I couldn't go through that, again."

Hezekiah and Howard both wanted to take a trip to Montana and beat the hell out of Nantan's father. Nantan didn't know that they all knew what his father had done. And none of them had approved.

~

Mark saw that Hezekiah and Howard were upset and decided to ease the tension. "Hey, Dad, you wanted to know when I learned how to shoot pool?"

"Yeah," Floyd said.

"Meet the master!" He pointed at Geno. "This boy taught me everything I know about the game. I paid my way through college from the knowledge I got from him."

"You hustled your way through college, Mark!" Floyd frowned. He really didn't know a thing about his son. When he and MeiLi offered to pay, Mark had refused, saying it was taken care of. They'd assumed he'd gotten student grants and loans.

Mark laughed. "Yup!" He didn't even have the decency to be embarrassed.

Floyd shook his head. "Shame on you, Son!"

Ram stepped around Symphony and raised his hand. "Excuse me. Can I have a word with you, Geno?"

Everyone started laughing.

~

Sal, Geno and Nantan were given rooms in the wing with the single guys. Ali and Destiny picked a suite on the couples' end.

Doc examined the women's ears to make sure no damage had been done. He told them in a day or so everything would be back to normal.

Just like Ali had predicted, the women whisked Destiny away, to catch up and get her acclimated to her new home.

~

Lara and James were visiting Ali, in his new room. Lara was a hormonal mess. "I am so happy for you," she cried.

Ali started laughing. "Get a towel, man," he told James. And Lara started laughing.

"I almost screwed up, Lara. I didn't know Antonio had told his hit men where Geno lived," Ali confessed to her.

"But if you had not been there, Nantan would have been killed and we never would have known." Lara started crying all over again. "None of us knew he was in Indiana all this time. His family abandoned him..." She sobbed. "...Like we did Jodi."

"Girl, how pregnant *is* you, anyway?" Ali laughed.

Lara hit him. "I *are* three months!" she said, just as grammatically wrong as he'd been. He knew she'd been an English Professor and it irked her when people didn't speak correctly. He was not only James' best friend. He was hers, too. They'd already decided he was this baby's Godfather.

"James, I feel sorry for you, man."

"Leave me alone! I can't help it."

"My Goddaughter better not come here a big cry baby," he teased.

They all started laughing.

CHAPTER 3

Ali and James joined the other men in the pool room. As expected, Geno was teaching Arak the art of playing poker. "This game isn't as much fun as Bid Whist," Arak complained.

"Why?" Chaz asked. He'd been standing around the table watching.

Mark laughed. "Bid Whist is a game of strategy and you have a partner; that is Arak's specialty. Poker is more like life."

"How so?" Ali asked.

"You're on your own. You gotta play the hand you're dealt," Mark said. Then he looked at Geno. "You gotta know when to fight and when to duck for cover. What to keep and what to throw away."

Geno knew Mark was talking about the people trying to kill him and Sal. And the decision they'd have to make. He nodded his head.

Chaz started laughing. "There's no wonder Arak doesn't like Poker. We don't run, do we, brotha?"

"Not on your life!" Arak gave him a fist bump.

"We ran today," Nantan said.

Brock shook his head. "Not really."

"What would you call it, then?" Nantan asked. Once they'd landed in the kitchen, Nantan had stood back against the wall and observed Brock. With his naked eye, he saw *all* of Brock's hidden powers. "You could have thrown up a shield, and that bomb wouldn't have hurt anyone in that house."

Brock frowned. "How could you, possibly, know that?"

"My second sight allows me to see beyond your wildest imagination."

Brock stared at him for a moment, and then just shook his head. "So, you have to know the enemy was watching, too."

Nantan nodded. "I presumed as much."

"If that house blew and we were all still standing they would have known something unnatural had happened," Brock said.

"You would have exposed our trump card,"

Sal said.

Brock nodded his head. "This way, you guys are alive, and well." Then he smiled. "But your enemies don't know that."

"They also don't know that they have just acquired a legion of new enemies," Ali said. "When they came after you guys, they unknowingly came after my 'lil Darlin'. That was a colossal mistake."

"You're willing to fight with me, and my father?" Geno asked.

"First we are going to find out who are the traitors, in your organization," Brock told Sal.

"I no longer have an organization." Then he looked at his son. "This is our one chance to get out. I want to take it, Son. I want to live the remainder of my life in, quiet, reflection. I want peace and to make peace, with my Creator. What about you?"

"Not, necessarily, quiet reflection. That's for old folks. But I would like to not have to look over my shoulder, every minute of every day. I'd like to not worry about someone trying to kill you. I'd like to stop calling you 'uncle'," Geno said, and they smiled at each other. "I'd like to stop living the double life, and just be me...Dad."

"So you don't want revenge against the people who blew up your house?" Brock asked.

"No. They think they've won. If it looks like we're running, then so be it. My son tried to kill me. I don't have much pride left. Let them have this false victory," Sal said.

"That's fine and good, but I have a score to settle," Ali said. "It's too personal for me."

"And me," Doc said.

"And me," Batman said.

"My family was in that house, but they had no way of knowing that, because we were teleported in. Just like they didn't know you were there. I'm with Sal," Luther said. "None of us were hurt. If you go after them, Sal will feel compelled to, likewise, do so. Let the man turn his life around."

"I'm afraid he is right. I pulled your family into this battle. If you go after them, I will be honor bound to fight with you," Sal agreed.

~

Geno walked over and put his arm around

Ditto's shoulder. "Speaking of turning your life around, you'll never guess who I saw?" he asked, with a half smile.

"Who?" Ditto asked.

"Naomi."

Ditto's facial expression went from relaxed, to pained. His voice trembled. "Where?"

"She came by the house looking for you, about a month ago."

"A month!"

"Yeah. She quit her job and moved back to town. For some reason, she missed you." Geno smiled.

Ditto forgot anyone else was in the room and shoved him against the wall. "A month! I could kick your sorry ass!" he yelled at his friend, and slammed his fist into the wall. "How could you do this to me, Eugene?"

"Did I say a month? I meant this morning." Geno kept smiling. "Man, you, still, got it bad for that woman!" He reached in his pocket, took out a piece of paper and dangled it in Ditto's face. "Want her number?"

Ditto snatched the paper from Geno's hand.

"Screw you, man." He turned around to see all the men staring at him.

"Well! Well! Well!" Howard said, smiling from ear to ear. "It looks like that pretty little girl's got you hooked, son."

"So what if she does," Ditto said, embarrassed. He could kill Geno for forcing him to expose his emotions. He'd done everything, but crawl through glass, begging Naomi not to go. But she'd left him and he'd gotten sloppy drunk and cried. Geno knew that, too. Damn him!

"So what happened?" Hezekiah said.

"She broke his heart when her job transferred her out of the country. He asked her to stay, but her career was important to her. More important than he was, or so she thought. But, the girl's been miserable, without him," Geno volunteered.

"Shut up, Eugene!" Ditto barked. He stared at his friend and dared him to say another word.

"She came by this morning, while Ali and Sal were gone. She told us she'd made a mistake, Howard. She was afraid to go by your house. She was afraid you'd reject her, so she came to us for help," Nantan said. The four of them had spent a lot of time together. He liked her and Howard together; they were meant to be. He'd seen the ties that bound their souls together the first time he saw the two of them together. "She misses you. She still loves you, man. Don't let your wounded, pride get in the way. She's waiting to hear from you."

Brock was reading Ditto's mind. The woman had crushed him. Brock knew how he felt. "How do you get past the hurt?"

Everybody looked at him. The team knew what he was alluding to, but the Walkers didn't have a clue. Brock was good at hiding his feelings. "He asked the woman not to leave and she did, anyway. She put her job before him. How does Ditto trust her not to decide to leave again, for whatever reason?"

"When SnowAnna left me-"

"Cutie left you!" Brock cut him off.

"Yeah, she left me. She took my kids and moved back to Montana with Lightwings. She stayed gone for a month," Hezekiah said. "At first I had too much pride to ask her to come back. I was hurt, but I was miserable without my wife. So I drove to Montana, prepared to get on my knees and *beg* her to come home."

"So what happened, Grandpa?" Addis asked. "Did you have to beg Grandma?"

"When I got there, she had never even unpacked. She'd missed me, too."

"But how did you get over her leaving you?" Ditto asked.

"You have to make a choice…Pride or happiness. I loved her too much to let her leave without fighting to get her back. I still do."

"Cindy didn't leave me. She tried to make me leave her, though," Howard said.

"Say what?" Henry asked. He didn't know his parents had ever split up.

"She kicked my ass out in the middle of the night! Then, the next day she changed the locks on the door and changed our phone number."

"What did you do, Dad?" Ditto asked.

"It's been so long ago, I don't remember. You boys were little tots. Hope wasn't born yet."

"How did you win her back?" Brock asked.

"Shit, I slept in my car, in the driveway." Everyone started laughing at him. "I ain't shame. I ain't ever had foolish pride, when it came to

Cindy." Howard laughed. "Have you guys seen my wife? No way in hell, was I going to lose that woman. After about a week, she got sick of me begging to come back in. One night she cracked the door open and walked away from it. I eased my black butt back in. She'd put a blanket and pillow on the couch and went back to the bedroom…and closed the door! I slept on that couch for about a week. I didn't care; I was back inside the *house*! After that, we talked and everything was okay. Hope was, prematurely, born seven months later." He winked at Chaz.

"Sasha and I never split up, per se. But, you know, we were married seven or eight years before we had Leroy. The first five or six years we were enjoying each other and weren't trying to have a baby. Then when we decided we were ready, it wasn't happening. We were trying hard, but couldn't get pregnant. Sex on demand, instead of spontaneous, takes the romance out of it. That's hard on a relationship. I think she wanted to leave me, but her family had disowned her, for marrying me; she had no place to go. We started sleeping in separate bedrooms and not speaking to each other.

That lasted for about two or three months. I was miserable! Don't get me wrong, I love my children, but I wouldn't have cared if we never had any. I loved that sassy little woman. I was hurt because I felt like she didn't want me, if I couldn't give her children. We finally talked and she said she wanted to leave me, so I could find someone who could give *me* children. She thought something was, medically, wrong with her, not me. We decided what was going to be, was going to be. We loved each other too much to walk away. Once we stopped trying and just started enjoying each other, again, Leroy popped up." He laughed. "After Leroy, all I had to do was look at that sassy little Russian and she'd get pregnant."

"Amanda's and my marriage was almost destroyed because of that no good Ted. But I fought like hell to save it. I wasn't going to lose my family," Justin added.

"Yeah, that was a bad time for us," Aden said, and his brothers nodded.

"MeiLi and I never had any problems, but I've counseled enough couples to know this much-you gotta ask yourself, can you bear to see her happy with someone else, Ditto? If the answer is *yes,* then she's not your wife. If the answer is *no,* you need to swallow your pride and go reconcile with your woman."

"So Leroy, what about Lilith? Can you stand to see her with someone else?" Luther asked.

"Yeah." He was honest. Three years with Lilith, and he just didn't feel what Ditto felt for Naomi. He cared about her and he enjoyed the constant companionship, but he didn't love her.

"Thank God!" Aden said. "I'm telling you that woman ain't right."

~

Batman decided to help Brock out. "So, Elijah, you felt like Sasha wanted kids more than she wanted you?"

"Yeah."

"So after the kids were born, did she put them ahead of your relationship?" Batman asked.

"Yeah, but they all do," Elijah answered honestly.

"Seriously?" Chaz asked. He hadn't felt like Hope was doing that. They both took care of the boys and saw to their needs. But there was always plenty enough time for just him and her.

"Yeah, it's a mother/child thing," Hezekiah said. "But then, so did I. It's no longer about the two adults in the room, but the children." Again, his mind went back to his father and how he always put him and his brothers first.

"Does it bother you guys?" Batman asked.

"No. How can you object to your children having a good mother?"

"It's always been a source of pride, for me," Howard said. "I picked a good woman to mother my children. She gave up *everything* for them."

"Every single time I look at my sons, I fall in love with Lara...all over again," James added. He even sounded smitten.

"So none of you ever felt slighted?" Brock asked.

"At first you experience that jealousy; it's only natural. But you get over it when you see the emotional strength your children are developing, from their mother's nurturing."

Nurturing! That's the key. Jodi was nurturing their nineteen year old daughter. The team had given her whatever, the hell she wanted.

But, they hadn't nurtured Aurellia, because they didn't know how to. Brock closed his eyes and shook his head. This was helping, but Jodi still threatened to leave him. It was one thing to leave and go to your father's house, but a whole other thing to go to Paradise. There was no peace to be had over this situation. He'd have to learn to live with it. "So what are you going to do, Nephew?" Brock asked Ditto.

But Ditto was nowhere to be found. He'd eased out of the room while they were having their discussion. He wasn't going to front. He loved that girl and he was going to get her back. He still carried her engagement ring in his pocket, everyday. He quietly prayed, *'please let her say yes, this time.'*

"I guess we know where's he's gone." Howard laughed. "Wait 'til I tell Cindy." If he was right, they would have a new daughter-in-law very soon.

~

Everyone started playing cards and shooting pool again. Nantan wanted to have a private conversation with Elijah. When he saw him off by himself, sifting through the CD's, he approached him. "Can I ask you something?"

"Sure." Elijah knew what he wanted.

"Did Aunt Sasha ever get over her family turning their backs on her?"

"Probably not, but she's never regretted her decision. It came down to what was more important, their happiness or hers. You can't live the life someone else wants you to live, and be true to yourself. In the end no one is happy; because you'll resent them for making you choose."

"I do resent them. I was twenty-one when they kicked me out of the house and off the reservation. I had no money and nowhere to go. My father told me if I ever set foot on Montana soil again, he'd kill me."

Elijah stopped looking at the CD's and frowned. "Kill you! So what did you do?"

"Destiny gave me what little money she'd saved, and I struck out on foot with no direction in mind. I was homeless for a few years. I would call Destiny from time to time, just to hear a familiar voice. She told me when E-du-di found out what my parents had done, to me, he disowned my father. He told my father he was the disgrace, not me. E-du-di came to get me, but I refused to go back because I couldn't handle the humiliation. So, E-du-di found a decent place for me to stay. He paid for me to go to college. He and Destiny were all I had."

"Why didn't you call your Aunt SnowAnna?"

"I saw the hatred in my parents' eyes. They vilified me, throughout the community. And my older sister jumped on their bandwagon. If they wouldn't accept me, I had no reason to believe Aunt Snow and Uncle Hezekiah would. I made E-du-di promise not to tell anyone, but Destiny, where I was."

Elijah smiled. "But you found out, tonight, that they would've accepted you, didn't you, son. We all would have."

"Why couldn't my parents be open minded? They almost destroyed my life, Uncle. It was friends, like Ditto, that helped me see I was okay, just as I am."

"Here's the thing." Elijah sat on one of the bar stools and motioned for Nantan to sit. "Most people claim they are disgusted and offended by pornography, yet their minds always seem to end up in the gutter." He and Nantan both laughed. "Me personally, I never think about what consenting adults do behind their, closed, bedroom doors…gay or straight." Then he pointed at Hezekiah. "H is my main man. Our bond goes deeper than most. I know everything about him. He and SnowAnna have three daughters, right?"

Nantan nodded. "Yes."

Elijah frowned and raised his right hand. "I swear to God, I'd go blind if I tried to envision what that crusty ass did, with SnowAnna, to produce those girls."

Nantan wasn't expecting him to say that and burst out laughing. He'd tried to get people to see that he was more than gay, but what he was really saying was, what I do in the privacy of my bedroom, is my business. Elijah had just articulated what he'd been trying to say. "Damn Unc, that's it!"

Elijah saw Nantan was finally relaxing, so he kept going. "See, me and Hezekiah, we shoot the shit together, always have. We fight for and with each other, always will. But when I go to my bedroom, the last damn thing on my mind is what the hell he is doing in his! You feel me, Son?"

Nantan was rolling. "So in other words, your imagination ain't that vivid!"

"Hell Nawl!" Elijah said, emphatically, and they both burst out laughing.

"Thanks, Uncle. You don't know what you've just done for me. You have made me feel welcome here. I was afraid that even though everyone was smiling in my face, they were still scrutinizing me."

"No one is, Son. We care about you, as a person. Not what you do behind your closed door. There are a lot of families and children here. We are respectful of everyone's privacy. Now, I don't want to see you and Eugene groping each other, but I don't want to see Brock and Jodi doing it, either. That stuff belongs in the bedroom."

"That's all I've ever wanted, was for my parents to care about me. To love me, for the person I am. It's like when I look at Sasha, I don't see a white aunt, I just see my aunt. That's the way I wanted them to see me. Not as their 'gay' son, but just their son. Why couldn't they do that?"

"Listen, your parents are wrong; but you can't make someone accept you. You can't help how you feel and neither can they. Are *you* happy?"

Nantan smiled. "Yes, I am."

"I'll bet your parents aren't." Elijah winked at him. Then he said, "But you have to forgive them."

"Why?"

"For you. As long as they can control an emotion…they control you, Son."

Nantan nodded his head. He knew that was true because he'd thought about them every day, for fifteen years. One moment he'd be laughing, and the next minute, morose. Whenever he'd accomplish something big, he was always tempted to call them; in hopes that that one thing would make them proud of him. They didn't know how successful he'd become. He'd wanted to share his financial success with them.

But more than anything, it was the isolation from family. Thank God he had that in abundance, now. He looked forward to telling his aunts and uncles of his many accomplishments. He *needed* somebody to be proud of him. He needed his father, Hezekiah, to tell him he was a *good* man. He smiled at Elijah. "You're right."

Elijah smiled. "Listen, if it doesn't work out with ole crusty butt, I'll be honored to be your father."

They both laughed. Nantan felt something he hadn't felt, in years…like he belonged!

CHAPTER 4

The women were in the kitchen, having their own little 'hen' party. Chef agreed to let them fix their own dips and snacks. Destiny fit in like she'd always been there. She'd showered and borrowed one of Lillian's outfits because Ali had told her they'd be going out later. Lillian had told her to take as many as she liked, because she was pregnant and would soon not be able to wear them, anyway. Then Lillian said, "We're all pregnant."

SnowAnna was still upset with her. "Destiny, you knew all along that Nantan was living here, in Indiana. Why did you not let me know?"

Destiny thought about the night her parents kicked Nantan out. Nantan had just turned twenty-one. Even though he was tall, he was, measurably, much smaller and thinner than he is now. Her father was big and muscular, like E-du-di. He and Nantan had argued about Nantan settling down. Since Nantan was their father's only son it was his duty to carry on the family name. Nantan had refused, saying he didn't want any children. But their father kept pushing. Finally Nantan told his parents the truth…he was gay. Their father hit him in the face over and over, with his fist. Nantan had been respectful and didn't strike back. But his words cut to the core, *'your beating me won't change the fact, Father, that I am gay.'* Their father hit him again, knocking him down. Then he kicked him in the side. Destiny had stepped in and stopped their father from kicking him again. *"Leave him the hell alone!"* she'd shouted and caught her father off guard.

Their mother had been even worse. She'd called him a pervert and said he was *not* her son. They'd kicked him out the house that night, with just the clothes on his back.

She wouldn't further humiliate Nantan by telling these women the whole sordid details. If he wanted to, at some point, it was his story to tell. "I couldn't, Aunt Snow. He couldn't face another rejection."

"I wouldn't have rejected him! I was upset with your parents when I found out what they'd done! Your father and I have not spoken, much, since that time. He didn't like the things I said to him." SnowAnna frowned. Her brother had bragged to her about beating his son. "That self righteous bastard!"

"I have no love loss for my parents, especially my mother. I would never allow Ali to alienate my children. I moved in with E-du-di, that night. When I told E-du-di what happened, he was livid. You know he's bigger and stronger than my father. E-du-di hit my father so hard he went flying across the room. My father landed head first into the sofa table. E-du-di stood there, with his arms folded, daring my father to get up and hit him back. My father knew he couldn't beat E-du-di, so he didn't even try to get up. E-du-di finally said, *'It don't feel good being bullied, does it! You went to great lengths to bring that boy into this world. Until Nantan is welcome in your home, you are no longer welcome in mine!'* He, and I, walked out my parents' house and have never gone back."

"I'm just glad he's here," Lara said, wiping her eyes. "Your mother is a bigger disappointment, to me. I can't see doing that to any of my boys.

And I damn sure wouldn't allow James to! He knew if he ever laid a hand on my children I'd light his ass up with buckshot."

"I told Justin when he experienced his first labor pain, he could whip my boys. And not until then," Amanda added. She was equally upset with her uncle's wife. She refused to call her, her aunt.

"I'm happy that you all have embraced my brother. I don't know what would have become of me and Ali, if you hadn't," Destiny said honestly. "I will never stay anywhere Nantan is not welcome."

"Have you and Nantan always been close?" Symphony asked her. She was a little jealous. Hope was close to her brothers, Robyn was close to hers and now Destiny and her brother was close. She'd missed that type relationship with her brothers. She committed, in her mind, to get closer with Matthew and Mark.

"Yes. I was born seven months after him."

"Seven months?" Symphony frowned.

"Yes. It should have been nine months, but I was two months preemie. We were raised like twins."

"I was having a fit about being pregnant, with my babies only being four months old," Jodi said.

"He's always been my best friend," Destiny said, with a smile.

~

Ali walked into the kitchen while the ladies were still talking. He'd waited as long as he could to get her away from them. "Excuse me, ladies." He smiled. "I need to steal Destiny. We have a date."

"I am still angry at you, Ali." SnowAnna frowned.

He walked over and kissed her on the cheek. "Don't be mad at me, 'Cutie', I had to make sure it was okay for Nantan, Geno and Sal to come. All's well." Then he put his arm around Destiny and vanished.

~

Ali and Destiny walked in the bistro and the maître d' smiled. "It is good to see you, again, Ali."

"You too, Pierre." This was his favorite place to eat. He came here at least once a month. Each time he came, he'd envision himself here with his 'spirit' mate. He'd always known he'd bring her whenever he found her.

Pierre escorted them to a secluded table in the back, next to a floor to ceiling window. Ali had called ahead and requested this seating arrangement, for two reasons. He wanted the privacy and he wanted to be able to teleport out if trouble came. The waiter brought them a menu and Ali's favorite wine.

Destiny had never been to such a fancy place. She gazed out the window and smiled. "The view is breathtaking, Ali," she said a little too loudly. The restaurant's back appeared to be up against the river. Then she noticed ships sailing in the distance. She frowned and looked across the table at, a smiling, Ali. "This is not Indiana. Where are we?" She tried to whisper, but it didn't work.

Ali reached out and unblocked her ears. He tilted his glass of wine towards her. "Italy."

"Italy?" If she could have afforded to travel, this was the first place she would've come. How did he know?

Ali's smile got bigger at the expression on her face. "Italy."

"WOW! I've never seen any place but Indiana and Montana and all the cities in between." She looked back out the window. That wasn't a river! "Ali, that's the Mediterranean Sea?"

"Yes, it is. Do you like the view?"

"It's lovely." The lights from the cruise ships made it that much more appealing.

"We will see it all, Darlin'. One date at a time."

She almost choked. "I hope you don't plan on making me wait that long."

He laughed, because he knew what she was talking about. "I doubt I can hold out that long."

The sun had gone down and Ali had removed his glasses. She was starring into his beautiful dark eyes. "Just being with you is enough, but this is spectacular."

"The night is still young." He smiled, cryptically.

They spent the next hour dining and enjoying each other's company. They weren't trying to mimic the couples he'd seen in the park. Secluded away from the other guests, they found their own groove. Ali really was a romantic. She wondered if she'd ever get tired of the way he treated her. Probably not.

They were lost in each other's eyes when someone teleported in at Ali's back. Destiny jumped. He looked familiar to her. For some reason she wasn't afraid.

Ali's eyes turned red for a split second. He was already holding Destiny's hand and tried to teleport her out, to safety; but couldn't. He was locked in place. Enraged, he prepared himself for battle. He stood up and just before he turned, he heard, *"Examine your actions, boy."* He turned around and came face to face with his mentor.

"She does not know me. Be careful what you say."

"Kobabiel! What are you doing here, man?" Ali embraced his forearm, and gave him a, one armed, gentlemen's hug.

"I should be asking you that! You are in my playground, Dawg," Kobabiel informed him. *"It pleases me, Ali, that you are my granddaughter's mate."*

"I've been wondering where you were stationed." Ali slapped him on the back. "Have a seat." *"Man, I'm so pleased with my mate I could do a holy dance".*

Kobabiel sat down and smiled at Destiny. "I am sorry to interrupt your dinner, but I had to come and visit with my friend for a minute."

Kobabiel was no longer Indian. He was Italian but Destiny saw the resemblance. They could change their nationality, but not their features. "You look so much like Hania Lightwings, you could be his son. Do you know him?"

"I won't lie to my mate," Ali informed him.

"Yes. I do know Spirit Warrior. He is a fine man," Kobabiel said, hoping that would be enough.

"Are you related to him?" Destiny pushed. This man looked more like her grandfather than her father did.

"I am," Kobabiel responded.

Destiny was about to ask how he was related, when she saw Hania walking towards them. "What is my grandfather doing here? And how did he get here?"

Ali and Kobabiel both turned around. Kobabiel stood and extended his hand. "Spirit

Warrior."

Hania grabbed Kobabiel's forearm. "Good to see you, Father."

"Father!" Destiny frowned.

Hania extended a hand to Ali. "Thank you for looking after my grandson. I knew you would welcome him into your home. I understand my daughter is upset with you and me." He started laughing.

"Yup, pretty much." Ali smiled.

"Well, I have a saying…what you don't get over, you die with." He laughed. "She'll get over it."

"How did you get here?" Ali asked.

"A friend brought me."

When Hania went to hug Destiny she pushed him back. "Did you call him 'father', E-du-di?"

"Yes, I did, child."

"Why? Is he a Priest?"

They all laughed at her. "Have a seat, child."

Ali and Kobabiel sat quietly listening to Hania explain their family history to Destiny. He told her how old he was and that her Aunt Snow had always known. He further explained that the women at the house had been told everything a week ago. "However, they have not met my father. Not even SnowAnna," Hania informed her.

"What about my father. Does he know our heritage?"

"No! I've always known your father was not trustworthy. Look at how he told the entire community about your brother. He made sure his son had no one to turn to and no shelter on or off the reservation. It was uncalled for and petty. I am ashamed that I didn't teach him better." They could hear the disappointment in his voice.

Hania was feeling like a hypocrite, because he'd chastised Brock for attacking Deuce, even though he had attacked his own son. His only excuse was he wanted his son to see how it felt to be abused by someone more powerful than he was.

"It's not your fault, E-du-di. You can't take the blame for my father's heartlessness."

Kobabiel felt sorry for his son. He knew the story and had told Spirit Warrior that his son had free will. He even understood why Spirit Warrior had hit his son, even though he never would have himself.

"So does Aunt Snow know that you are still alive?" Destiny asked Kobabiel.

"I am sure she does. We will not die until that glorious day. But I have not had a role in her life," Kobabiel told her.

"Why have I been privileged?"

"My intentions were to come and visit with my friend, Ali. I failed to realize how much I and my son look alike. You are quite perceptive."

"Are you going to visit the estate to see the twins?" Ali asked. "Your granddaughters are remarkable."

Kobabiel and Hania both stood up. Kobabiel grabbed his son's arm and said, "In due season." Then he teleported them both back to Montana.

Ali heard one last request, *'Do not keep my granddaughter away from home too long, Ali.'*

~

Ali and Destiny finished their 'cold' dinner and then he took her *sightseeing.* He teleported them to the Colosseum, and told her the history of the ruins of Roman civilization. They walked, hand in hand, through the cobblestone streets of Italy and climbed the Spanish stairs in Rome. He took her to the Leaning Tower and even Vatican City. It was amazing. He was amazing.

Ali took Destiny on a shopping spree at a dozen boutiques and designer houses. He bought her everything from shoes to scarves to sexy lingerie. Everything he picked out was designer, even the jeans. She'd never owned anything that cost this much money.

She tried to protest. "Ali, this is too much!"

"Your clothes were destroyed when they blew up Nantan's house. I will not have you wearing your cousin's clothes. It dishonors you if I don't provide for my 'spirit' mate."

When he picked up a flannel nightgown she laughed. "You'd be satisfied with me wearing that?"

"It's practical. You can't always come to bed in skimpy clothing. I won't, Darlin'."

Ali gave their address to all the boutiques for them to ship the merchandise. He and Destiny carried a few choice packages with them. But he didn't want his arms overloaded to the point where he couldn't keep one hand on her.

Then he took her to a jewelry store and

together they picked out their wedding rings. They agreed on a three carat marquis diamond, with eternity stones that wrapped around a platinum gold band, for her; a matching band for him with three small diamonds. They waited while the jeweler engraved "Destiny's mate" in his and "Bezaliel's mate" in hers. When the jeweler handed the rings to Ali, he caressed her cheek, in front of the other customers. "I have waited for you a long time. Will you marry me, Darlin'?"

Destiny shook her head. "No."

The jeweler gasped and started sweating; those were thirty thousand dollar rings he'd just engraved. "No refund!" he shouted. "You should have settled this before I engrave. No refund!"

The other customers were embarrassed to have witnessed this. They tried to turn their backs, but curiosity got the better of them. They felt bad for Ali.

Ali looked at Destiny and smiled. "Don't make me beg. I've waited a long time for you, Darlin'."

Destiny started laughing. "I love you, Ali. I can't imagine my life without you. I will marry you."

He placed the engagement ring on her finger and kissed her. He placed both bands in his pocket.

All the customers and the jeweler started clapping.

~

Neither of them wanted the date to end. They were standing along the waterway, kissing. "So when do you want to get married?" Ali asked.

"Whenever you want to, Ali. I only have Nantan and E-du-di. I don't want my parents there. My sister, either. They will upset Nantan."

He'd clearly heard what Hania said. Her father was not to be trusted. He was about to tell her it was fine with him if they didn't come; but he felt the stain of something so evil, he swore he smelt sulfur. Without explaining, he teleported them both back to the estate.

"What happened?" Destiny asked. She saw the expression on his face.

"There was something out there. Something more evil than I've ever experienced."

"What was it?" She thought she felt him tremble.

"I don't know," he answered, but he was concerned about Kobabiel. "I'm sorry our evening ended so abruptly but I need to speak with Brock. I'll make it up to you, Darlin'."

"I had a wonderful evening, Ali. There is nothing to make up," Destiny assured him.

He tried to remain calm as he escorted her to their suite. He'd been in such a hurry to get her back to the estate, he didn't think to teleport directly to their suit. "I'll be back shortly." He kissed her, and then went to find Brock and the team.

CHAPTER 5

Ali found the men, still in the poolroom. He walked in and grabbed Brock by the arms. "Search my mind! Tell me what you see?"

Brock frowned. If he didn't know better he'd swear Ali looked frightened. "What happened?"

Ali squeezed Brock's arms and shook him. His voice squeaked, but not from laughter. "Search my damn mind, Seraphiel!" He was frantic and reeked of fear. "Tell me what you see!" He squeaked again.

Everyone stopped what they were doing and moved in closer. None of them had ever seen Ali rattled. The boy was trembling.

Brock started searching Ali's mind and he took the team with him. He didn't know where to start, so he started from the time Ali left the poolroom, for his date. Damn the boy was a romantic; who knew he had it in him. Brock wished he'd had enough time to do those things with Jodi, in the beginning. He smiled when he saw his friend Kobabiel. He saw them pick out their wedding rings and thought, *'Damn this boy is classy'*. He saw Ali and Destiny standing along the waterfront discussing their wedding plans. Then he smelt 'IT'! He felt 'IT'! And finally he saw 'IT'! He, forcefully, shoved Ali away from him. "How in the hell?"

The team members were staring, in confusion. They'd smelt, felt and seen everything Brock had. And it scared the crap out of them.

That thing gave Chaz the hebbie jebbies. He started rubbing his arms, trying to warm the chill bumps. "What in the *hell* was that, man?"

All the other team members jumped back and shouted, "Ooooh!" All of them were unnerved. They'd never seen anything with a face like that. Demons, for the most part, were, exceptionally, attractive.

"I could have spent the rest of my life not knowing something like that, even, existed." Batman frowned. "Where the *hell* did that thing come from? The water?" He'd evidently watched too much TV.

For a minute they all felt hostile towards

Brock. They had an, unreasonable, urge to attack him for exposing them to that creature. Its face was lopsided with bulbous infectious boils that seeped a rotten smelling odor. Its eyes were completely black and sat far apart. They had no lids and they were filled with rage and contempt for everything in its path. It didn't have a nose, just a gaping hole that had maggots crawling in and around it. Compared to that creature's face, Brock had looked like a prince when he'd revealed Seraphiel's true face to them.

Ali was relieved that he wasn't the only one that had been unnerved by the thing. He vigorously shook his head, trying to get the image out of his mind's eye. "What the *hell* is that, Brock?" he squeaked.

"HATRED!" Brock answered. He felt it taking a hold of his men.

"HATRED! How did he escape?" Ali squeaked. He'd never seen him before tonight, but knew what he could do.

"I don't know, but he has," Brock answered.

"Is Kobabiel going to be okay over there?" Ali asked, concerned about his friend.

"Yes," Brock said, and stared at Ali. "Hatred followed you *here.*"

Ali staggered backwards and shouted, "What!" But he knew Brock was telling the truth, because he was feeling what all the others were feeling... Intense animosity!

"Release them and get the hell out of my house!" Brock roared and pushed Hatred's spirit back outside the estate.

Everyone heard Hatred angrily growling because Brock was holding him at bay with his mind, alone.

Brock turned around. "Where is Ditto? Is he back, yet?"

"No. What's happening, Brock?" Howard asked, now concerned for his son. He'd felt the same rage the Watchers had felt. "Is my son in danger?"

Brock reached out and spoke to Ditto. *"Where are you, Nephew?"*

"I'm on my way back to the estate. What's wrong?" Ditto heard the urgency in Brock's voice.

"Are you alone?"

"Yeah. What's wrong, Unc?" Ditto asked.

The hair on the back of his neck stood up and he had a sense of trepidation. He needed to get home, now! He slammed his foot on the gas, pressed down on the clutch and shifted to fifth gear. He'd gone less than a quarter mile when, a thick density of fog appeared, out of nowhere. He slammed on his brakes and the car skidded, sideways, to an abrupt stop. *"Something's wrong, Unc!"* Then he heard something, growling, outside the car. He turned, looked out of the window, and screamed, "UNC!"

"Hold on!" Brock couldn't wait for Ditto to get somewhere secluded. He teleported him to the poolroom and his Jaguar to the estate grounds.

~

Ditto was still in the sitting position, when he landed in the poolroom. Eugene and Nantan kept his butt from hitting the floor, but his knees were wobbly and he went down, anyway. "What was that thing out there?" he asked, trembling. "What that hell was that thing, Unc?" Howard and Henry helped him to his feet, but he was shaking like a leaf. They had to help him stay on his feet. He wanted to cry. "You gotta tell me what, *the hell,* that was! I'm never going to be able to sleep, again!"

Normally Brock functioned with just a thought...but not tonight. Tonight he was as animated as Mark. He had the appearance of a maestro, as he slung his arms and hands, putting up a maximum shield around the estate. He repeated the process, several times, placing shields on top of shields. They would not be able to even open the doors. No one was getting out...and nothing *evil* was getting in.

In that same, animated fashion, he erected a cone of silence around the *entire* estate. They would be able to hear from room to room, but no one and *nothing* could hear anything going on inside the estate.

Then he silenced everyone's pulse and heartbeat, so the vibration could not be felt by the demon. Finally he made everyone inside the estate, invisible to prying eyes.

~

No one had ever seen Brock this frazzled, not even when Samjaza had attacked. Whatever the hell had scared Ditto had also scared Brock. They were all afraid. "Are the women safe, upstairs?" Hezekiah asked.

"Yes," Brock calmly said, but it was obvious his attention was divided.

"What is going on, Daddy?" Ditto asked, sounding like a little boy. "What the hell was that thing?" He was rubbing his, goose pimpled, arms. He was too damn big, and too damn old, to sit on his father's lap...but he wanted to. He wanted his daddy to assure him that there were no such things as monsters. Hell he wouldn't mind sleeping with his 'daddy' and 'mommy', tonight.

~

All of the cousins saw how frightened Ditto was. He hadn't called his father 'daddy' since he was twelve! He was the toughest one of them all, including Lara's sons. If he was afraid and the team was afraid, they were screwed. They all eased up close to their own fathers. Nantan was all up under Hezekiah.

The Walker men, James and Justin, knew it was time to shore up their courage. Their sons, although grown men, were frightened. They didn't know what they were up against, but they'd fight, to the death, to protect their families.

~

Brock called out for his leader, "Michael!"

Michael did not respond.

"Michael!" Brock called again.

He still didn't respond.

"DAD!" Brock shouted.

~

Everyone noticed the look on Hezekiah's face. Brock had never once called him dad. He didn't mind sharing his son with Michael, but he couldn't bear to hear Brock call Michael what he'd never called him. Everyone felt his resentment intensifying.

"Keep your feelings in check, H. Now is not the time. These demons will seize on your emotions!" Brock shouted at him. "Pull it together, Old Man!"

"DAD!" Brock shouted one more time, knowing it was for naught. There was only one reason Michael wouldn't answer *his* call…

~

Gabriel appeared in Michael's stead. "Seraphiel, heed your own warning! Ease your spirit, boy!" Then he calmed Brock's nerves.

Brock turned around. "What's going on, Gabriel, where is Michael!"

"He is doing battle. Azazel found a portal and he has unleashed a legion of his malevolent demons: Hatred, Revenge, Malice, Resentment, and so on. We need you, and Yomiel, on this one. Satariel is fighting, as we speak, in his own territory. Kobabiel is in Montana, fighting."

"But those things have always been around," Hezekiah stated.

"Their spirits yes, but not the demons, themselves," Gabriel said. "With the demons loose, their spirits are magnified, a thousand fold."

"Are they strong enough to penetrate my shield?" Brock asked. He wasn't going anywhere, if they were. Those demons were no match for him, but the humans in this house could be consumed with their spirits. They could force these people to turn on each other.

Gabriel reached out and increased Brock's shields and the cone. Then he looked at Ali. "Your 'spirit' mate's father helped them escape. They are after her, Nantan, Kwanita, Jodi and

SnowAnna. They have already attacked Hania in Montana."

Hezekiah's heart skipped a beat. "Is Lightwings alright?"

Before Gabriel could answer, Kobabiel teleported in with his son, Hania. Hania looked worse for wear. There was no doubt he'd been through the wringer. Hezekiah and Nantan reached for him. "E-du-di, are you alright?" Nantan asked.

"I killed my son, tonight," E-du-di whispered. "I killed my son." Then he looked into Nantan's eyes. "I killed your whole family, Nantan. Forgive me."

Nantan didn't know how to process that. His family had turned their backs on him, but they were still his family. In his heart, although hurt, he still loved them. "What happened, E-du-di?"

"They came, to my home, to kill me. They were filled with hatred because I stood by you. They hated Destiny for standing by you. Your mother heard SnowAnna say she was your mother now. She hated her. Your sister saw your cousins embrace Destiny, and hated her for it. After they killed me, they were coming for all of you. Your father helped Azazel release Hatred, and Hatred consumed them all. There was nothing of my son left, but Hatred!"

"Did you not see this coming, E-du-di?" Nantan asked. He knew how powerful his grandfather's second sight was.

"Yes."

"Couldn't you have prevented it, this one time?" Nantan asked, sounding like a child.

"The last time I attempted to rob Fate of her due, I wounded Mother Time. Little Wolf suffered her wrath. Kwanita's mother and father died, as a consequence," he finally admitted out loud. "I could not offend Fate or Mother Time, again."

"He could not prevent it," Kobabiel said, defending his son's lack of action. "Life's hand has to be played." Then he teleported back to Montana.

The Walkers were too concerned about Hania to realize that they had just met his father.

Ali realized that Hania had brought Destiny to Indiana because he *knew* what was going to happen. He'd gotten her out of harm's way, but not himself. Kobabiel had even tried to warn him earlier, in Italy… *"Do not keep my granddaughter away from home too long."* Had she still been in Montana they would have killed his mate. NO! Not killed, but harmed her. Michael would not have allowed them to kill her. What he'd felt, in Italy, was Hatred trying to get control of his emotions. But Hatred could not gain purchase of him because, at that point in time, all he'd felt was love, in abundance.

"Seraphiel, you must clear your heart of any resentment before you fight," Gabriel said. "Any crack in your defenses and you will lose this battle."

Brock nodded. He was thankful Gabriel hadn't said 'towards Aurellia'.

"Destiny is mine to protect. I will not hide behind these walls and let Brock fight my battle," Ali said. "We are a team. If he goes, I go!"

"Word!" Chaz, Dan and Batman said at the same time.

Arak and Ram had already reached in the air for their battle axes. Yomiel was standing at his brother's side. He didn't say a word, but his posture spoke volumes. Even if he hadn't been an

Ultimate Watcher, he would go with his brother. Nobody would harm his gift from God. Brighteyes was his to protect.

"This battle will not require physical strength. There is no need for your battle axes," Gabriel informed them. "This will be a battle like none you've ever fought. The minute you show any signs of aggression...you lose. That is why we only wanted Ultimate Watchers. They have more control over their emotions, than you guys. All around the world only Ultimate Watchers are fighting tonight."

"Since you have explained the rules of engagement, we can handle it," Ali assured him. All the other team members nodded their heads.

"First thing I need everyone to do is gather up your families and meet me in the basement. I don't want to teleport them down there because the demons will feel the pulse," Brock informed them. "Also, no one tell Destiny, Kwanita, or SnowAnna about what happened in Montana. We can't afford the emotion right now."

Everyone agreed.

~

Everyone, automatically, went to the Chapel. The women were scared to death. The men were protective. Again, Brock noticed that Chef had possession of Lorraine and her girls. He didn't have time to examine it, figuring she was the only single woman there and he wanted to make her feel protected, too. Henry and Ditto had Sarah. Richard was in a wheel chair being pushed by JR. He and Jodi were holding the babies and Deuce had possession of Aurellia. "Come with me," Brock said.

He took them through a door that they all assumed was just another room. Once everyone was inside, Arak sealed the door and the lights came on.

Everyone turned around and just stared. The damn room was as big as the west wing of the estate. It came equipped with a food pantry, a refrigerator, dozens of beds, a big screen TV. Ram had even insisted on putting a pool table in here, once he'd learned about the game. There were a dozen bathrooms, each with large, walk in showers. The walls, ceiling and floors, were all made of reinforced titanium. And, it was sound proof.

Brock started to explain. "We don't know how long this will take, but I have put up a shield around the estate so no one will able to get in. I have also put up a cone, so they will not hear you, either. The demons we will fight tonight are 'principle' demons. They are passive aggressive and will not attack you physically. But they will attack your minds, in search of your weaknesses. They will latch on to whatever emotions you are feeling and intensify them. Their sole purpose is to cause you to fight and destroy each other. I need everyone to release your fears, anxieties, jealousies and any other negative emotions. If any of you have aught against someone, you have to air your differences now. As long as you keep positive thoughts, you all will be safe. Be at ease and trust your love for one another." Then he turned towards Ditto. "How are things between you and your woman?"

Ditto was still nervous over what he'd seen, but smiled. "We're good." Then he frowned, damn if he didn't feel like a coward. "Is Naomi safe out there?"

"Yes."

Brock kissed Jodi. Unfortunately, there was no time for a private conversation. "I was hurt that you chose Aurellia, over me."

Jodi looked confused, and frowned. "What are you talking about, Brock?"

"You said you wouldn't stay with me, if she didn't."

"I *never* said that. I'm *never* going to leave you, Brock. Why would you think...that?" Then she remembered. "Oh. I'm sorry, Brock, I didn't mean to hurt you. Why didn't you say anything?"

"What was there to say? It is obvious that you're staying with me is dependent on Aurellia staying."

"That's not true. That...is...not...true!" Jodi adamantly denied. She wrapped her arms around him. "I just didn't want my family to be split up. I love you too much to *ever* leave you, Boo. I love Aurellia too much to let her go."

Brock stroked her cheek. He still couldn't believe how fortunate he was to have her. No other woman could have ever humbled him enough to pour out his fears. "I love you, Dimples, I always have. I won't be worth a snow shovel in a hurricane, if you leave me."

Then he told Aurellia, "I resent the way you manipulated your mother. You knew all along that you were never going to leave. Through no fault of your own, you are a spoiled, little, brat. Your actions crushed me, Baby Girl."

Aurellia started to cry. "I'm sorry, Daddy. I just don't like anybody being mad at me. Please don't be mad at me, Daddy."

"I love you, Baby Girl. I'm not mad at you. You say you don't want to be treated like a child, but your actions prove otherwise. If you plan to marry, one day soon, you have to grow up. Just because someone is mad at you doesn't mean that they don't love you, okay. What you did is what those demons outside are trying to do. You can't truly love someone and manipulate them, too, Baby. People have to be free to feel what they feel; without the threat of being abandoned."

"H, I know it stung for you to hear me call Michael 'dad'. He has been my dad for almost four thousand years, but you are my *'father'.* I need you to understand that neither title diminishes the other. He has his place in my heart and you have yours."

One by one everyone started confessing their feelings. Lara told James she was hurt that he'd kept that secret from her all those years. She told Deuce and Aurellia that she was still upset with them for what they'd done. Then she told them that she loved and forgave them and that their punishment was over. Jodi agreed.

Hezekiah told SnowAnna he was hurt that she'd kept a multitude of secrets from him, for over forty five years, but he loved her, anyway.

Addison confessed that he was jealous of Deuce and Aurellia. But he added he knew she wasn't his wife. If he couldn't have her, he was glad Deuce could.

All the Watchers confessed that they'd been upset with Jodi for hurting Brock. Then Ram said, "He's looked for you forever. For you to want to leave him, with Aurellia, was, devastatingly, cruel, Babe." Ram was the only one who could have said that to Jodi, because he loved her, as much as Brock.

"I'm not leaving Brock," Jodi told them. "I'm sorry if that's what you all thought."

The one that caught everyone off guard was

Matthew. He confessed that he'd had a thing for Kwanita for years, but since they were cousins it was a moot subject.

Everyone started laughing.

Yomiel laughed and said, "I leave her in your care, while I'm gone, but keep your hands to yourself, Dawg."

Kwanita blushed; she knew Matthew used to flirt with her all the time, but didn't know he was serious. It wouldn't have made a difference anyway because her heart had always belonged to Yomiel.

Ali kissed Destiny and smiled. "It is on nights like this that you can feel comfortable wearing a flannel nightgown. I will be too tired for anything, but sleep, when I return."

Destiny hugged him. "Just remember how much I love you, Ali. Hold that thought in the forefront of your mind and heart."

The team all kissed their 'spirit' mates, broke their links and walked out the room. They didn't want to teleport from the basement, because it would give the demons an idea that someone might be down there.

Arak had shown James how to reseal the door, once they exited. Once he resealed it he turned around to see a sea of troubled faces. He laughed. "C'mon now, at least it isn't that old creepy…dark castle."

Everyone started laughing, remembering how scared the women had been. The ones who had not been there wanted to hear the stories. Before long they were all laughing and telling the tale.

Mark ushered Floyd and Sal to a far corner and whispered, "We are the two or three, gathered together."

Both Sal and Floyd understood and nodded their head. Sal was glad to be counted in that number.

All three started praying.

CHAPTER 6

The 'principle' demons, too evil to cross the threshold, were gathered outside the gates. Brock knew they were scanning the estate, searching for humans that they could manipulate. By placing the humans in the panic shelter, they could not be seen or sensed. The titanium prevented the ultra violet heat waves, of their body temperatures, from being seen. He'd had that room built right after he bought the land. He'd known even back then the strength of titanium. His mind had always been planning for the day they found their mates.

~

Brock and Gabriel were right; this was a battle like none they'd ever experienced. They weren't sure they were equipped to handle it, either. This was a battle of wits. Mind to mind...Emotion to emotion. Who would break first?

Michael had reconfigured the portal, where

the demons could enter but not exit. He, Gabriel and Raphael were busy forcing demons into the portal, but thousands had escaped. The demons were trying to fight them but couldn't compete, because they had no emotions for the demons to attack. But each malevolent demon had thousands of little imps at their beck and call.

~

Revenge, Malice, and Resentment were even more hideous, to look at, than Hatred, although not by much. Ram started laughing, "If I looked like you guys, I'd be pissed too."

The team watched as Revenge bombarded Ram's mind with what had happened to Symphony. Ram's facial expression changed from laughter to outrage. He wanted blood and he wanted it now! "Bring them back, so I can kill them again, Brock." he shouted.

Brock shook his head. "Get it together, Ram. Don't let them win, Dawg," Brock said, very calmly.

Malice attacked Ram, showing him scenes of being tossed into hell. "You bastard! Why did you leave me down there that long?" He tried to hit

Brock.

"Think Ram, think. You and I have no issues with each other. You're my right hand man and my best friend, Dawg. They are playing games with your mind, man!" Brock responded. Then he flooded Ram's mind with images of them standing back to back; fighting for and with each other.

Ram shook his head. "Dang!"

~

Malice attacked Arak; and showed him his days in the internment camp. But Arak just laughed, "Ain't no Germans here, you freak! I love every one of these guys, so try again!"

And try Malice did, but nothing worked on Arak.

Resentment took a shot at him by letting him see that he was one of the last to find his 'spirit' mate. "Floyd knows who she is, why won't he tell you?" Resentment taunted him. "Make him tell you who she is."

Arak turned to walk back towards the estate, but Ali caught his arm. "Nah man, don't do it. You know why."

Arak shook himself. "Um. Thanks, Dawg."

~

Resentment attacked Batman, next. "Your mate was shot to pieces, while Chaziel's got away scot-free. Why didn't he help your mate?"

"Yeah, why didn't you, Chaz?" Batman growled. He started walking towards Chaz like he was going to attack him.

Dan grabbed his arm. "Come on man, fight it. You know he didn't know who she was."

~

One by one these 'principle' demons attacked the team. And one by one they had succumbed, only to have their team mates pull them out of it. This went on for hours and hours. This emotional battle was wearing the team down. Each of them realized a physical battle was much easier, than battles of the mind.

"Your brother was living the life while you were being chased by your other eighteen brothers," Malice said.

"Yeah, I know. But that's life," Doc responded.

"He could have helped you eons ago," Resentment added.

"He's helping me now," Doc responded.

"Don't you want Brock to bring your brothers back so you can show them how powerful you are now? Don't you want to kill them, yourself?" Revenge shouted.

"Nah, dead is dead. I'm cool." Doc smiled. Doc was cool, because he really didn't harbor any hatred, malice or resentment towards anyone.

Revenge dropped a boat load of snow on Yomiel's head. Yomiel just brushed it off. "It won't work, freak."

Well it damn sure worked on Brock. He went crazy. "Get that damn snow off him!" he shouted. His eyes turned red, with rage. He grabbed Revenge by the throat and tossed him across the field.

"That's right!" Revenge laughed. "Get revenge! They buried your brother in an avalanche! Do something about it!"

Brock was growling, "I'll kill those bastards!"

He started to teleport, but Doc caught him. "Look at me, man. I'm good. They can't hurt me."

While Doc was helping Brock, Hatred attacked Chaz. He showed him his mother.

Chaz growled and attacked Hatred. Hatred was laughing and Resentment joined in. He showed Chaz his father laughing, while his mother was dying.

Then Revenge and Hatred showed them all of their mothers' death. They showed them scene after scene of things that had affected them, in their past.

The team lost the battle. They all went crazy.

~

Hatred grinned. While they were fighting, amongst themselves, he was testing the shields up against the estate. There was fresh meat he needed to destroy beyond those shields. He needed to get inside. No one noticed him easing towards the estate. He couldn't enter the gates, but his spirit could.

~

Inside the panic shelter the humans were doing fine. They had not been attacked and thought it was because they were properly protected.

The men were shooting pool. Geno was teaching them the skill of hitting more than one ball at a time. He and Mark had tried to play against each other, but he'd trained Mark too well. Every time Mark got the cue stick he'd sink all the balls. Every time Geno got it, he'd do likewise. It wasn't any fun. The Walker men were impressed with Mark and Geno.

~

The women were all admiring Destiny's engagement ring. She was telling them about her romantic trip to Italy. She told them about the sights and the shopping spree. She told them Ali was romancing her; and how much she loved it.

~

The babies started screaming for attention. Jodi picked them up and tried to rock one on each of her shoulders, but they kept screaming. When they'd gotten, mostly, everyone's attention they spoke. *"Your 'spirit' mates, sons and brothers are losing the battle,"* Elizabeth said.

Mark missed every ball on the table. Geno dropped his cue stick. Everybody in the room, gasped. They had no idea these babies could communicate.

Deuce shouted, "I knew they were laughing at

me! I knew it!"

They all circled around Jodi and stared at the babies.

"They need the power of your love, to help them," Hannah added.

Hezekiah reached and took Elizabeth from Jodi's arms. He stared into her eyes. "Show Grandpa, Baby."

Elizabeth flooded all of their minds with the scene from just outside the gate. *"They have closed their links, to everyone, so they can't feel how much you love them. They are powerless, without it,"* Elizabeth added. *"All they can feel is Malice, Revenge, Resentment and Hatred."*

"Can you open the link, Baby?" Jodi asked. Brock was in terrible shape and he needed her. "Let mommy talk with your daddy."

"Of course we can open the links. We are our father's daughters!" Hannah said, and then giggled.

"Hush, Hannah. This is no time for fun and games," Elizabeth scolded her. Then she looked around the room at all the eyes watching her. *"Opening the link won't be enough. They are too*

far gone. We will teleport everyone to the battlefield, but you can't show any fear towards the creatures."

"Let them see them now so it won't be a shock to them," Hannah suggested.

"Good idea, Sis," Elizabeth said, and showed everyone what the creatures look like.

Ditto jumped. "That's the thing that was trying to get in my car!"

"Damn!" Floyd cursed. "Sorry."

The babies laughed. *"That's alright, Uncle Floyd,"* Elizabeth said.

"Could you love me, if I looked like that, Mommy?" Hannah laughed again.

Jodi laughed. *"I'm just glad you don't, Baby."*

"Me too. You can't buy enough makeup to fix those faces." Hannah kept laughing.

"Hannah!" Elizabeth scolded her once more. It was obvious to everyone that Hannah would be the playful one. She'd be the one who would find humor in every situation. Elizabeth, on the other hand, would be serious, in nature.

"You too bossy, Girl, chill!" Hannah said,

and everyone started laughing.

"You can teleport all of us?" Hezekiah asked, Elizabeth.

"Of course. Hannah's right. We are our father's daughters."

~

The team knew they'd lost this battle. Hatred, Malice, Revenge and Resentment were having a field day with their emotions. They felt it, but couldn't stop it. They'd never felt such intense, negative, emotions in their entire existence.

It wasn't supposed to be a physical battle, but Hatred had taken control of their emotions. Not only were they fighting the demons, they were fighting each other. Once the gap was in their emotional defenses; the demons were able to flood their minds with past conflicts they'd had against each other: The fight in the conference room, Ram hitting Dan, Chaz out of control on the front porch, Ram hitting Brock, Brock letting Ram hit Dan, and Batman wanting to fight Brock. On and on the demons kept attacking, and intensifying, their emotions.

Michael, Gabriel and Raphael couldn't help

them; they were too busy ushering the demons back in the portal. Michael locked them down, so they could not teleport into hell. If they went down they would not be coming back anytime soon, because for the time being, a trip to hell was one way. He removed all of their special powers, like Chaz's ability to Phantom. He also kept Brock from becoming Seraphiel to keep him from killing his team. They'd get over fighting each other, but they would not get over fighting to the death!

~

They all felt it at the same time. A tidal wave of love that was so pure, it took their breath away. They, and the demons, stopped fighting and looked around. Across the field their family was walking toward them...all fifty nine of them; their 'spirit' mates, and children, leading the way. It was the most awesome sight they'd ever seen. Their families had abandoned the protection of the panic shelter to come and rescue them! It brought tears to their eyes. They looked at each other, smiled and then looked back at their family.

~

The opposite of Hatred, is love! It is the

greatest, and most powerful, of all emotions. Hatred screamed, as love encompassed him. It felt like someone was heaping hot coal on his head. "NO!" he shouted and started to back up.

Malice started trembling and actually fell over his own feet. Kindness and friendship were his archenemies and they were walking towards him, en masse. His legs were too weak to get up, so he started, vigorously, crawling towards the portal. Every now and then he'd nervously look over his shoulder to make sure they weren't catching up to him.

Revenge actually ran towards the open portal, trying to escape his nemesis…Forgiveness! One day he was going to kill that spirit. But not today! He jumped in the portal taking all of his, revengeful, imps with him.

Resentment tripped over Malice, while trying to flee. He kicked him in the face for being in the way. Affection and happiness were his arch-rivals, and these humans reeked of it.

~

"Leave our daddy alone!" Chaz's boys shouted. They had their fists balled and shook them at the demons.

"You better run, you old ugly thing!" Jason said, and jumped in Chaz's arm.

"Want us to beat them up for you, Daddy?" Jonathan said, standing in front of Chaz, like he was protecting him. Then he shouted at the running demon. "And you bet' not come back, neither!"

Hope picked Jonathan up and wrapped her arm around Chaz's neck. "I love you, Baby. You alright?"

"You tell me," Chaz choked out. His boys weren't scared of those ugly creatures. They wanted to protect him!

~

Robyn jumped up in Batman's arms. "I love you, Big Daddy! I wasn't even afraid! Now give me a piggy back ride."

~

Kwanita jumped in Doc's arms. "Are you alright, Yomiel?" He didn't look as bad as the others, because he'd held out as long as he could. He didn't start fighting until Ram hit Brock. Then it was on. Nobody got away with hitting his brother; not even his brother's best friend!

~

Symphony jumped in Ram's arms and he grunted. Doc had knocked the hell out of him after he'd hit Brock. He'd bet money, Doc hit harder than him. He'd like to test that theory one day, but who could they hit? "Angel, look at your beautiful face." She started kissing his bruises.

~

Ali opened his arms for Destiny and grunted when she jumped in them. Arak packed a mean punch. "It's definitely flannel tonight, Darlin'. We should have bought a heating pad."

"I love you Ali." Destiny wrapped her arms around his head. "I'll give you a massage when we get to our room."

Nantan, Geno and Sal all embraced him. He was their family and they loved him, too.

~

Mark grabbed Arak and hugged him. They were best friends now. "Hey Dawg, did you get those bruises from friend or foe?"

Arak laughed and flinched. He didn't know why Dan hit him. "Both. How bad does it look, man?"

Mark laughed. "Pretty bad. I wouldn't try to find my mate until the swelling goes down, if I were you."

~

Desiree was all over Donnell, hugging and kissing his bruised face, too. "My sweet baby, don't ever shut me out again. You know you can't survive without me."

~

Lillian and Dan were hugging and kissing, ready to get their freak on. Dan was hurt...but not *that* bad!

~

Baraqiel found himself being hugged by Amanda and Lara, each not wanting him to be left out. Each one kissed a side of his face. "Until you find your mate, we will be her stand in," Lara said, and they laughed at the expressions on their husbands' faces.

~

Ditto beat Jodi to Brock. He was crazy about his Uncle and knew he was Brock's favorite. He wrapped his arms around him. "Hey Unc, you alright?"

"Yeah, nephew it was rough for a minute, though." Then he reached for Jodi. He didn't love anybody as much as he loved this girl. "God, Jodi, you see, now, how much I need you? Promise me you won't leave me."

"Never gonna happen, Boo." She kissed his bruised face. "That ain't ever gonna happen."

Brock frowned, remembering he'd broken the link. And his shields were so tight they shouldn't have been able to open the door! "How?"

The babies started kicking and giggling. Brock looked at them, then at Jodi and then started shaking his head. "No," he said, in disbelief.

Jodi nodded her head.

Hezekiah put his arm around his boy. "These are some powerful little girls, we got here."

"They teleported *all* of us out here, Wolf," SnowAnna said, and kissed him.

Brock kept shaking his head in disbelief.

The girls kept giggling and laughing.

Aurellia jumped in Brock's arms. "I love you, Daddy. I don't want to be like those creatures. I'm going to do better, I promise."

"I love you too, Baby Girl." He hugged her tightly and kissed her cheek. "I love you."

Then he reached for Hannah and looked in her eyes. "Did you rescue Daddy?"

"Yeah. But Elizabeth is a big ole meanie, just like you." She started laughing and kicking her legs.

"Hannah!" Elizabeth scolded her, again.

"See, just a big old meanie!" She, and everyone, else started laughing.

Everyone was still laughing as Brock let Elizabeth and Hannah teleport, them all, back inside the estate.

~

"Do you guys ever wish you had human emotions?" Gabriel asked Michael and Raphael. They'd stood, unnoticed, in the yard and watched 'love' take control of the situation.

"No, but next time those bastards escape I say we just bring the humans and leave those sorry Watchers in the house!" Raphael said and teleported away.

"What about you, Mike?" Gabriel asked.

Michael didn't answer. He'd already opened

himself up to feeling human emotions. Not the negative kind, but love was taking control of him. Love for everyone in that estate. "I need to go have a talk with Azazel. Would you like to come?"

"Wouldn't miss it," Gabriel replied.

They teleported to the dungeon far below the bowels of hell.

CHAPTER 7

Destiny started to run a bath for Ali to soak his bruised muscles, but he stopped her. He told her that her immediate family was coming to talk with them, first. He didn't want Hania to tell this story more than one time. Hezekiah, Doc and Brock agreed with him. Hania had not gone to the panic shelter with them, because he wasn't sure he'd be able to pull it off. He'd, secretly, remained in his room upstairs. The women didn't even know he was in the house.

~

Destiny had an ominous feeling in the pit of her stomach. She didn't have second sight, but she knew something was wrong when Nantan and Geno refused to look at her. She looked at Ali, for answers, but he just squeezed her hand.

Two by two her relatives piled in the room: SnowAnna, Kwanita, Jodi, Amanda and Lara, and all of their mates. The women were all wondering what was going on. The men were all stoic.

Finally, the door opened, one last time, and Hania walked in. He did not move towards them, but stood still, at the door. All of the women smiled, glad to see him, until they saw his face.

~

SnowAnna didn't need the façade of a 'vision quest'. Not this time. One look at her father's face and her hidden powers burst through, like Yellowstone Park's geyser, 'Old Faithful'. She released Hezekiah's hand and slowly stood. Everyone watched as, she grimaced, and her eyes clouded over.

Her daughters reached for her hands, and at the same time said, "Mama?"

But she snatched her hands away from them. They watched as she, blinded by her second sight, took measured steps, towards Hania. She was moaning, and holding her chest, as the tragic scene was unfolding, in her mind. She heard, what she knew was her brother's, demonic, voice:

"You chose that pervert, Nantan, over us!" her brother shouted.

"Yes, I did," Hania responded.

"We've come to kill you, you old fool," her sister-in-law bragged.

Hania stood firm, with his arms folded. "You can try."

"Then we're going to kill your precious, Snow Anna and her three bitches," Her niece shouted, and then started laughing. "I meant witches!"

Her brother growled, "Snow Anna can't have my son!"

"You did not want him. You humiliated him in front of the community. You dared him to come back to Montana," Hania said, calmly. "Nantan is Snow Anna's son now."

"He's possessed by the devil! He has to be sacrificed!" Her sister-in-law

shouted. "So his soul can be saved, you old fool."

"It is not his soul that is in danger of Hell's fire. I will not allow you to harm Nantan!" Hania responded.

Her brother laughed. "You won't be able to stop us!"

SnowAnna covered both her ears as she heard her niece's voice. It sounded like the shrill of a possessed, banshee:

"We are going to gut those treacherous demon loving witches, Jodi, Destiny and Kwanita! We know they are all brides of the devil!"

Then SnowAnna watched, in horror, as the three of them spread out, getting ready to attack. Her pulse started to race. She hadn't noticed, before, that they had weapons. They all had demonic smiles and were making god awful noises.

The scene reminded her of a pack of hyenas stalking a great buffalo. But her father didn't move an inch; not his head and not his body. She moaned, but couldn't get out of the vision. The next scene showed:

Hania's son attacked him, with an iron pipe. His daughter-in-law stabbed him and his granddaughter jumped on his back trying to take him down to the floor.

Even though wounded, he pulled his granddaughter over his shoulder and tossed her across the room. Then he took the knife from his daughter-in-law's hand, tossed it out the open door. All the while, his son continued to beat him, with the iron pipe.

Hania tried to take the pipe from his son, but the two women were on his back, again. Both, with knives in their hands, trying to slit his throat!

SnowAnna watched, in fascination, as her father fought off his attackers. He never moved from the spot where he was standing. He reminded her of a tree, with strong roots. But she knew he couldn't last for long. He was an old man, compared to these hateful people. She appeared to be in a trance as she continued to watch:

Hania forcefully tossed the women off him again and again; all the while trying to get the pipe out of his son's hands. He wasn't trying to hurt any of them, they were his children. He wasn't showing any aggression, he was just stopping them from attacking him. But that pipe was taking a toll on him.

SnowAnna stopped, abruptly, and screamed when her brother hit their father, again. "NO!" She heard the sound when it made contact. He couldn't survive that! She watched as he stopped tussling with the women:

Hania went down. He'd moved too slowly that time and the pipe caught him in his left temple.

Snow Anna's knees were wobbling, straining to hold her up. She looked like she was on a tightrope, as she eased towards Hania. Hezekiah tried to support her, but she pushed him away. She had to get to E-du-di. She had to get to her father.

In her mind she was in the house, with her father. She was swinging her arms, trying to get them off of him. "Father!" she shouted. Tears were streaming down her face and she was hyperventilating, as the next scene unfolded:

Hania, now down, had reached his maximum, passive, tolerance. He didn't mind dying; his heart was broken, anyway. But, if they killed him they would come for his 'precious' little girl, grandson and granddaughters. But it was his love, for his only daughter, that was the driving force behind his resolve. He loved his little girl, too much, to let these evil people hurt her.

With a made up mind, and love in his heart, the decision was made...

SnowAnna heard her father's thoughts. She knew what he was getting ready to do, and why. It would bring even more sorrow to her father's heart. But her brother and his family had left him no choice. She was sobbing and trembling, as the next scene unfolded:

Hania rolled and propelled up like a Great White Shark, out of the water. His attackers went flying through the air. He caught his granddaughter, by her neck, and crumbled every bone. He threw her carcass on top of her father, pinning him down.

Then he grabbed his daughter-in-law's hand, twisted it. *"It is your black heart that had forced my son to turn on me."* In one violent move, he impaled the knife she was holding, to its hilt, through her heart. Then with laser precision, he turned it and sliced her heart in half. Enraged, he lifted her dead body over his head, and threw her out the large bay window; with enough force the entire frame fell out with her.

Hania turned, like a wild man, towards his son. He grabbed him by the collar, and yanked him up off the floor. He hesitated, for a moment, because he loved his son. He stared in his eyes, but his son wasn't there. There was nothing behind those eyes but, unadulterated, hate. Nothing would stop him now, his mind had snapped! *"You have destroyed me, Hatred!"* Hania said, with fury and contempt. He choked son's neck, with his bare hands, until there was no life left.

SnowAnna teetered on the balls of her feet, trying to stay upright. Her sister-in-law may have encouraged her brother to do these evil things, but he'd been a willing co-conspirator. The next scene validated her assumption:

Hatred jumped out of his son's body and smiled. *"Your son underestimated your strength, Spirit Warrior. When he summoned me, I told him we needed more than those weak women to defeat you."* Then he pointed to the dead bodies. *"Look at what you've done! You are, just, as evil as I am. You have killed three of your children, for the sake of one! SnowAnna doesn't love you. She left you in Montana, by yourself! She's known all along how evil her brother was! I could use a man of your strength. Help me kill Destiny, Kwanita and Jodi. They turned their backs on you and left you here, alone. Help me kill SnowAnna, Spirit Warrior!"* Hatred laughed and started moving toward Hania. *"Help me kill Nantan! None of them will want you after they realize you've killed your son."*

SnowAnna froze, in place. If Hatred got his hands on her father, he'd overtake his body; just like he did her brother's. "He lies, Father! I love you! You're the first man I ever loved! Don't let him touch you!" she shouted, and tried to get to him. "Don't let him touch you, Father!"

Then she saw a man enter the room. "HELP HIM!" she shouted. She'd never met him, but she knew who he was. He'd come to help! She smiled, through her tears, because her father wasn't alone, anymore. She listened to the sound of his command:

"You cannot have my son, Hatred. Release him and get out of his house!"

She watched as Hatred recoiled, at the sound of this man's voice. She felt, what had offended and frightened Hatred...this man's love for his son. Hatred fled! Her father was safe.

SnowAnna let out a sigh of relief and fell, unconscious, into her father's arms.

~

Hania had told the men that SnowAnna was powerful; that was how she'd been able to reach back two thousand years and contact Brock. It was evidenced now, because no one had to ask what happened. Once, the full magnitude of her powers were unleashed, everyone throughout the estate experienced her vision. It was as if a big movie screen was playing in every corner of the estate. There was no escaping this horrendous scene! Throughout the estate men, women, both young and old, and children were weeping. All of them were making their way to Ali's suite.

Hania held his daughter's unconscious body, cradled her head to his breast and cried. "I'm sorry, Daughter."

CHAPTER 8

Destiny screamed, "No! No! No!" Then her body went into convulsions. Her head was bouncing all over the place. She was shaking like she was being electrocuted. Ali could barely hold her. He couldn't take control of her mind or muscles. Brock tried, but he couldn't, either. Nantan was crying but trying to help hold his sister still, to no avail.

Deuce came running into the room. He wasn't sure if he should see after his grandmother or his cousin. When he saw Destiny he decided she was more urgent. He tried to give her a shot to calm her, but it didn't work.

She kept screaming, "No! No!" Then her eyes rolled in the back of her head and she laid still.

~

Ali had made a *big* mistake. He'd wanted to take his time, and romance her, so he hadn't claimed her. Now he couldn't help her, not without a blood connection. He should have known better.

Trouble always found a way to keep 'spirit' mates apart. He could read her mind but, he didn't have a solid unbreakable link with her, yet. If he had done right, he would have been able to cordon off her mind, anchor it to his and keep her sane. But he hadn't and right now her mind was slipping to a place he wasn't about to let her go.

This wasn't about the physical claiming. This was about holding onto what was already his. In front of everyone he exposed his teeth and sunk them into her neck.

~

Brock sensed what Ali was about to do. It was too intimate, an act, for on-lookers. He, preemptively, blocked the image from everyone's view, including his own. They saw Ali holding her, but they didn't see his teeth or see them make contact. He, only, appeared to be holding his head up against her neck, comforting her.

~

Ali drew on her blood and developed and a link, at the same time. *"Don't leave me, Darlin'. We'll get through this, together."*

"Ali, where are you?" She screamed. She

didn't know where she was. She couldn't find her way out of this abyss of darkness.

"Open you mind, I'm right here. Come back to me."

"How did I get here?"

"We'll talk about it later. Let your mind see my face. Let your mind come to my voice, Destiny."

She kept reaching for his physical body, but couldn't find it. It was too dark. *"I can't find you, Ali. Where are you? Get me out of here!"* She was frantic. *"It's too dark, Ali. Where are you? Come get me!"*

"I'm right here, Darlin'. I can't come get you. You have to reach for me, with your mind."

"How?"

"Remember how much I love you, Destiny. Remember how much I need you. Remember we are the only family Nantan has. He needs you now, Darlin'."

She remembered. *"Oh God, Ali! My parents were going to kill us. They tried to kill my E-du-di!"*

"Yes they did. But he's safe, now, and so are

you and Nantan."

"*I'm ashamed, Ali.*"

"*Why, Darlin'? You have done nothing to be shame of.*"

"*My parents, and sister, were, purely, evil. How can I look at E-du-di, again? How can I face Aunt SnowAnna? They were going to kill Jodi and Kwanita, too. How can I face everybody, knowing what my parents wanted to do to them?*" She didn't want to face them. It was better to stay here. She decided to embrace the darkness. "*Tell them I'm sorry.*"

"NO! DESTINY! NO!" He panicked and shouted out loud. "*Don't leave me, Darlin'! You'll face them with me, at your side. Nobody blames you. They are worried about you. Nantan is beside himself, with worry. Come on back, Darlin'. Stay with me.*"

"*What if nobody wants me around anymore? What if they think I'm as evil as my parents? Where will I go, Ali?*"

"*You will stay here with me. Nobody blames you, Destiny. Come on, come back to me. I need you, Darlin'. I've waited a long time for you; don't make me beg you to stay."*

She actually laughed. *"Like you were going to in the jewelry store?"*

"Yup, just like that. We have the rest of our lives together, Destiny. I have a lot more dates to take you on. I still haven't taken you to a movie. I want to take you on a picnic along the Serengeti Plain. I want you to see the Pyramids, in Egypt, with me. I was there, you know, when they were built."

"You were? What was that like?"

"Come back and I'll tell you. Come back, to me, please!!"

~

Everyone watched as Destiny's body relaxed and she wrapped her arms around Ali's neck. They all breathed a sigh of relief when she started to cry, in a normal, healthy fashion.

"You're alright, now, Darlin'." Ali was rocking her back and forth. "You're alright." He was trembling…that was too close. "I waited a long time for you." He whispered.

~

Hezekiah wanted to hold his wife, but her

father wouldn't let go of her. He kept repeating. "I'm sorry, my precious little girl." She could live to be as old as a Watcher and she'd still be his little girl. She was his first born and the love of his life. His wife used to complain, saying, *'You spoil that girl too much, Hania.'* He'd just shush her and keep right on spoiling SnowAnna. After SnowAnna they had five sons and one more daughter, Kwanita's mother. He never showed favoritism, toward any of his children, but he'd always loved SnowAnna, more. He pulled her tighter to his bosom, "I'm sorry, little girl."

~

SnowAnna began to stir. She knew it was her father holding her. She'd always know his touch. It had never changed in sixty years. He held her like she was a little girl and made her feel safe. "Father." She whispered. "Father. They tried to kill you." She started sobbing. She couldn't handle the way they'd all double teamed him and beaten him up. He loved his son enough to let them do it, to the point that he was willing to die. Then he thought about her being vulnerable to their attack. She knew what everyone else knew; he'd killed his son to protect her. She pulled away from him and started examining his body. "Are you hurt?" Then she yelled. "Get Deuce, those bastards stabbed E-du-di! They stabbed my father!" She started crying all over again. "They tried to kill my father!"

"I am well, little girl." Hania said and pulled her back into his embrace. "I am well, child."

~

Jodi, Amanda and Kwanita had been crying the entire time. Their sorrow so great, they were inconsolable. None of them were grieving for themselves, but for their E-du-di. None of them understood how their uncle could beat his, own, father with an iron pipe.

~

Lara was mad as hell. They'd planned on killing her mother and sister. She wanted to load up her shotgun and shot those dead bastards until that wasn't a stitch of their hides recognizable. She was tempted to demand that Brock bring all their sorry asses back; so she could kill them, all over again. The bastard! How in the hell could they judge anybody, she knew all their dirty little secrets! She'd kept their secrets, just as she'd kept James'.

~

Ditto came to check on his 'cousin'. Nantan was in shock. Eugene was trying to comfort him, but Nantan was just staring into space. Ditto knew his cousin and knew what that stare was about. He opened his arms and Nantan walked in. "This is not your fault, Nantan." Ditto said, patting him on the back. "None of this is your fault, man. We'll get through this together, just like we always have: you, me and Eugene."

How insightful. Destiny had only been concerned about herself. What about Nantan. She pulled away from Ali and walked over to her brother. "He's right, Nantan. This was about them, not you or me."

Nantan cried in Destiny's arms. In his mind it *was* his fault. From the moment he admitted he was gay, he'd brought nothing but trouble to their family. "I wish I could have been different, Destiny." He whispered.

All the cousins surrounded him, giving him the support he needed. "There's nothing wrong with you, Nantan." Mark said. "Nobody in this house feels like there is. You are a part of this family and we accept you just as you are."

"There ain't a damn thing wrong with you! Your parents were the ones that were sick!" Sam said. Everyone could hear the contempt in his voice. He'd been in the poolroom, when SnowAnna's vision had accosted him. His brothers had had to hold him down because he started literally tearing the room apart. His rage was out of control and he'd shouted, *"The sick bastards!"* He was like his mother, Lara, he wanted revenge. He wanted to summons their spirits back so he could have a go at them.

~

SnowAnna finally pulled away from her father. "You are *my* son, Nantan! I'm proud of you!" She and Hezekiah both hugged him. He, more than anyone, would need emotional support after this tragedy. To the very end, his parents thought he was perverted.

Sasha's family had thought the same thing about her. They'd even told her that they would have felt better if she'd lain down with a dog! It was she who got through to him. "Don't take responsibility for your parents, Nantan. My family disowned me, too. I haven't seen them in over forty years, but I've been happy all that time." She hugged him. "The heart wants what the heart wants, Baby."

~

Sal wasn't sure he had the right, to be there, but he certainly had the need. That scene was the most awful thing he'd ever witnessed. But he knew his son would have done the same thing to him, if given the chance. He knew exactly how and what Hania was feeling, because he was feeling the same thing. He walked over to Hania and patted him on the shoulder. "You and I have something in common. We both grieve over sons, who tried to kill us."

Hania closed his eyes and nodded. "Yes."

~

Nantan and Destiny walked hand in hand to their grandfather's opened arms. "I'm sorry." He said and hugged them. "I tried not to hurt your parents."

That was the truth. To the very end all he'd

done was protect himself. At any point he could have snapped them all in half, but he hadn't. Not until the end. "We love you E-du-di. You are all we've had for the last fifteen years."

"You, two, have a lot of family to support you, now. You no longer need me." He was weary.

"Yes we do. Don't go back. Stay here with us, E-du-di." Nantan begged. "I need you."

"We all need you." Hezekiah said from across the room. Everyone was nodding.

"Stay, Father. Let me take care of you." SnowAnna said starting to cry again. She hid her face in Hezekiah's chest, "They beat my father." She couldn't get past those three people, who were supposed to care for him, attacking her father. Yeah, he was a big man, but he was old. "Who beats up an old man?" She sobbed; and all the women started sobbing all over again.

Hezekiah wrapped his arms around her. "They were sick, Wife." That was the only answer Hezekiah could give her. He didn't understand it either.

Hania realized his little girl needed him to

stay. He didn't believe Hatred for a minute, when he'd said SnowAnna didn't love him. In fact she loved him so much that no one in the room, but him, knew what she'd done. Not even she knew. But she'd astral projected herself…through time and space! She was, actually, standing in the living room of his house, at the time he was being tempted by Hatred. She'd thought Hatred ran from his father, but she couldn't have been more wrong. Hatred ran from his little girl! What was strange to him was she had not ripped Mother Time's seam; nor had she offended her. His little girl had no idea, how powerful she was. "Brock, I assume-"

"I'll have to insist." Brock cut him off. Jodi was screaming, *"Make him stay! Make him stay!"* "This is your home, now." Then he spoke to Hania's mind. *"Do we need to clean up the scene in Montana?"*

"My father handled that. It will appear as though my son and his family left the reservation, as have I."

"What about your other, four, sons? Will they question?

"They do not live on the reservation. They

had no relationship with their brother. He didn't approve of their life styles either."

"Why?"

"They, like SnowAnna, married outside of our race. I didn't raise a bigot. I don't know where my son got that trait from. I think it was his wife. I knew she was evil from day one, but my son would not listen when I told him not to marry her."

"But we got Destiny out of the union, for Ali."

My grandchildren do not know this, but Nantan and Destiny were not her children."

Brock frowned. *"He cheated on his wife and she agreed to raise his children?"*

"After their first daughter was born, my daughter-in-law didn't want to carry any more babies. But my son wanted more children, especially a son. They agreed, together, that he could go outside the marriage bed, to father his children. Then the two of them would raise them. Destiny and Nantan are the results."

"Where's the mother?"

"Paradise."

The way he looked at Brock made him

curious. He reached into Hania mind…and frowned, again. *"You never told anyone?"*

"He was good to both children, when they were small. He was my son. I loved him, with all his flaws."

"You are a good man, Spirit Warrior. Your family secret is safe with me. You are not responsible for the road your son chose to travel."

"I am weary, Wolf. I killed my son, tonight. The pain is too great."

"I can ease your mind, if you'd like."

Hania nodded his head. Brock reached out and calmed him and filled him with the spirit of peace. *"Thank you, Wolf."*

~

SnowAnna insisted her father take the second bedroom in hers and Hezekiah's suite of rooms. Nobody objected, especially Hania. He loved his little girl. He needed time with her and her family to help him get over what he'd done. He was hurting inside, but he'd do it again and again. He'd never let anyone hurt SnowAnna.

~

Brock was holding in his rage over

SnowAnna's brother wanting to kill Jodi. He thought nobody knew, but Yomiel pulled him off to the side. "Let it go, Big Brother."

"What are you talking about, Yomiel."

"Boy, don't play dumb. They wanted to kill my wife, too. I know you want to take a trip to Hell. You gotta stop *doing* that, man. Besides, Hatred, Revenge and all their friends got a good whiff of you. They will recognize your scent the next time you go. They may lay a trap for you?"

Brock hadn't thought about that. But those bastards knew his weakness now...SNOW! Of course, he could easily change his scent and appearance, but he wouldn't reveal that to Yomiel. "Good looking out, Little Brother.

CHAPTER 9

Ali lay in bed with Destiny tucked close under his arms. She was still in shock and listless; like the walking dead. He'd had to bathe her and damn that was hard! For his own peace of mind he'd pulled that nice, flannel, nightgown over her head... it didn't work. She was still too sexy. She hadn't cried anymore, but had immediately slipped off to sleep, trying to escape again. Only this time he had control of her mind.

While he'd been trying to coax her back to sanity, he'd seen what her father had done to Nantan. And what Hania had done to her father in retaliation. He was grateful E-du-di had killed his son, because he, most certainly, would have if the man came anywhere near his mate or Nantan, for that matter. That would have created a strain on their relationship. They were safe now: Destiny, Nantan, Geno, Sal and Hania. They were his family and under his protective hand. He'd never let anyone lay a finger on either of them, ever again.

But for a moment he thought he'd lost her. SnowAnna didn't realize how powerful she was. She didn't realize, until later, that everyone was seeing it through her mind. Destiny's fragile mind could not deal with the scene, as it played out. She'd closed her mind and got the same affect one would get when they close their eyes...total darkness. It was the first time he'd ever experienced that and total darkness was frightening to him. Of course when he closed his eyes, to sleep, he got a glimpse of it but he usually fell asleep shortly thereafter. None of them closed their eyes for any length of time, until sleep took over, because none of them could stand the nothingness, of the dark.

But he'd been willing to face that nothingness to rescue his 'spirit' mate; to pull her out, before she got in too deep. His demon had encouraged him saying, *"Don't let her slip too deep, Dawg, or you won't be able to get her back. Do what you have to do."*

He and his demon had always had an amicable existence. It didn't want to be a demon, but it was what it was. He'd always considered it more his alter ego, than an evil enemy. Ali had promised his demon that he wouldn't exile it right away, because he wanted to romance his woman, first. His demon had promised, when the time came, he wouldn't fight. When the time came, Ali actually heard the creature say, *"Good for ya', Dawg...take care of your, little Darlin'."* Then his demon companion vanished. Strange as it were, he was going to miss him. He wished there was a way to save it.

He turned on his side and pulled Destiny closer. Just before he dozed off, he remembered that while he was buying Destiny outfits, the others didn't have any, either. He'd handle getting them suited up, tomorrow.

~

The Walker men were all in Hezekiah's room. They knew Hania wouldn't be able to sleep and wanted to be there for him. He'd been a father to them from the moment their father died. All of them were upset over his son's treatment of him. Floyd made a fresh pot of coffee and handed a cup to Hania. "Here you go, Lightwings."

"Thanks, Floyd," Hania's said, reaching for the cup, but his hand was trembling and he couldn't hold the cup. "I'm sorry, Son."

Floyd sat the cup down on the table and sat down beside Hania. "Is there anything I can do for you?"

"I should have let them kill me. It would have been easier on my spirit."

"I don't believe that," Floyd challenged him. He could the see weariness on Lightwings' face, but he also noticed the way he kept an eye on SnowAnna. He was still fearful for her. "If you had died, you would not have rested knowing SnowAnna would be in danger."

"I wasn't thinking." He looked over at Hezekiah. "I know my son-in-law would not have let anything happen to my daughter. I know you and your brothers would have stood with him to protect her."

"But you couldn't chance it, could you?" Floyd said. He knew that to be true, because he was a father. He would have laid down his biblical sword, gave up preaching the word and killed those bastards who attacked his little girl; if only he'd known who they were.

Hania shook his head. "No. I couldn't trust it. My son was a strong man. He was third generation Nephilim. None of you would have been able to protect her from him. I couldn't let him hurt my daughter with that damn pipe!"

None of them mentioned that SnowAnna was protected by the most powerful Nephilim, ever. Or that Brock would have killed his son, just as sure as he'd killed his own father, to keep his "*Cutie*" safe.

"You said that you were staying to see all the new babies, but that's not true, is it?" Floyd asked. "You stayed because you saw what danger was in store for SnowAnna."

Hania nodded his head. "I needed to get Destiny out of Montana. She'd come to visit me, like she always did. Her timing was bad, this time. I needed to get her to Ali. Michael would not let me bring her to this house, though. But then again, that was so that Nantan could be saved, also."

"When you said the demons were running rampart in Montana, had Hatred already escaped?" Hezekiah asked.

"Yes. But he didn't know where Destiny

was. My son didn't know either, so Hatred couldn't glean it from his mind, when he overtook his body. Michael took me to Italy, where my father, and mother, reside to get me out of harm's way. Imagine my surprise to see Ali and Destiny there."

"What? They were in Italy?" Howard asked. Damn that boy has class.

"Yes, he proposed to her there. My father and I sat and talked with them for a while. They make a fine couple. But, I had to go back to Montana to block my son. Otherwise, he would have come straight here."

"Goodness, that was your father that brought you here, wasn't it?" Hezekiah asked. All the Walker men frowned.

Hania laughed for the first time. "Yes, he looks young enough to be my grandson, doesn't he?"

"No joke," Howard said. But they shouldn't have been surprised; hell all their sons-in-law were five thousand years old, or there about.

Floyd noticed that Hania's hands had settled down and poured him a fresh cup of coffee. "Try this now."

It was the strangest damn thing, but coffee always made him relax. He looked around the room at all the Walker men. He knew why they were there. They were standing guard over him. They'd always been better to him than his son had been. He smiled. "You boys make an old man feel like he matters."

"You do matter, to us. You're the only father we have. We'd like to keep you around for a while." Howard frowned. "I wish you'd told us. We would have gone back with you...protected you."

"It wasn't your battle," Hania said, and stood. "This old man is tired, I'm going to rest a while."

Luther grabbed his arm. The two of them were the same height and build. "Let me help you to your room, Lightwings. I brought you something to sleep in."

Hania nodded his head. "You're a good man, Luther. But I sleep the way I came in the world," he said and then laughed, at the expressions on all their faces. Elijah had squeezed his eyes shut and shook his head.

SnowAnna laughed. "Father!"

"What?"

~

Ditto, the rest of the nephews, and Arak, were keeping Nantan occupied. This had been a terrible night for everyone, but especially for him. Unfortunately there was no way to block SnowAnna's vision, and he'd heard every mean spirited word his family had said. "I could offer you a drink, but you know it won't do any good. I learned that the hard way," Ditto said.

"Yeah, you did." Geno half smiled. He was worried. Nantan was more than his partner; he was his best friend, just like Ditto. The three of them had been through a lot together. When they could count on no one else, they always had each other.

"What happened?" Addison wanted to know.

"When Naomi left me, I got sloppy drunk."

Henry frowned. "But you don't drink."

"I did that night."

Nantan smacked his lips and rolled his eyes. "He had two beers and couldn't walk."

All the cousins started laughing at him.

"Two beers! What a wimp!" Matthew

laughed.

"It was more than two," Ditto said.

"It was two and a sip." Geno laughed. Then he got up and demonstrated the way Ditto had staggered, that night. "He was tanked."

Nantan finally laughed. "We had to put our boy to bed. He had the nerve to wake up, the next morning, with a hangover!"

They were all laughing at Ditto. He, once again, became the joke, only this time he didn't mind. "What are y'all laughing at Deuce and Addis? I'd better not ever catch either of you drinking. Don't ever mess with anything that will take control of your minds." Then he laughed. "Unless of course, it is a woman."

"My brothers and I can't have, so much as, a sip of wine," Sam said.

"Why?" Eugene asked.

Sam's brothers looked at him and they all nodded. "No more secrets," Tim said and they all agreed.

When Sam finished talking, Eugene looked at him and his brothers, then at all the cousins and said, in the most feminine voice, "Well ain't y'all special."

They all fell out laughing. Eugene was a hoot!

"I feel privileged, to be amongst the anointed." He kept at it.

Nantan stopped laughing. "If it had to happen this way, I'm glad I had all you guys here with me. I couldn't have handled this by myself."

They knew what 'this' was. None of them said anything; they waited to let him talk. But he didn't. He changed the subject.

"So what happened tonight, Howard?" Nantan asked. "With everything going on, I forgot you'd gone to see Naomi."

Ditto smiled. "I'm getting married, man."

"Does she know?" Henry teased his brother. But he secretly wondered whom he'd choose for the best man. Ditto and Eugene were, awfully, tight. He'd never been jealous of their friendship, but he'd be hurt if Ditto chose Eugene for his best man. He decided to tell himself that it wouldn't be him, just in case.

"Yeah, she knows. My woman loves me," Ditto bragged. Then he smiled at his brother. He knew what he was thinking. But he didn't have a cause to worry. Eugene and Nantan were his best friends, but Henry was his brother. Nothing would make him happier than to have Henry standing, at the altar, with him. "So get your, best man tux out, Henry."

Henry couldn't help but let out a deep breath. His big brother knew him well. He gave Ditto a fist bump, but he really wanted to hug and tell him how much it meant to him. He'd do that later when it was just the two of them.

"I'm happy for you, man." Nantan smiled. "I knew, all along, you and Naomi were going to end up back together."

"I wish you would have clued me in," Ditto said. "Man when she left me, I was screwed up."

"You think we didn't know that?" Eugene frowned.

"Yeah, that's why the next night when you showed up at our door, with that skank, I told her you were our third partner!" Nantan laughed. "Y'all should've seen her running out of our house." Everybody started laughing.

"The poor woman ran off and left her purse.

She texted Howard the next day and asked if he'd send it to her by courier." Eugene laughed.

"We never did figure out how she got home that night, seeing that she'd come to our house in Howard's car." Nantan kept laughing.

"That shit ain't funny!" Ditto pretended to be mad. "She told all her friends I was 'on the down low'! I couldn't get *any* action. She even put that shit on internet!"

"You weren't supposed to get any *'action'*. The only person who mattered knew the truth. Besides, you would have been using those women, anyway. How do you think Naomi would've felt knowing you'd become a 'ho' dog?" Nantan asked him. "Especially one day after the two of you broke up!" He didn't believe in sleeping around. His parents were hedonists; he'd seen them have swing parties and orgies, all his young life. It was disgusting. When he and Destiny got old enough they'd leave and go stay with their E-du-di for the night.

Ditto huffed. "But I didn't leave her! She left me! If I *had* slept with someone else, what could she have said?"

Nantan raised his eyebrows. "She could have said, "No" I won't marry you."

"Well yeah, there is that." Ditto laughed. "Good looking out, Nantan."

"How did you know that she was the one?' Addison asked, looking at Nantan.

"The first time I saw them together I could see the ties that bound their spirits. It was stronger than any I'd ever seen, until I saw Destiny and Ali. Then when I came here I saw all of our cousins and their mates and their ties were just as strong," Nantan answered.

"So what do you see when you see me and Aurellia, together?" Deuce asked.

"The same. You two are destined to be together. She's a beautiful young woman, Deuce. You will be very happy with her."

"I'm already happy, with her." Deuce smiled.

"Oh well, little brother. You might as well get over her." Aden teased Addison.

"Hey man, *don't* go there. Michael might show back up!" Addison frowned. He was so over his infatuation with Aurellia. Or at least he hoped he was.

"Who is Michael?" Nantan asked.

When they told him, he laughed. "Y'all really are special, aren't cha?"

"You, Sal and Eugene are, too. Can't you see that it was by design that you all are living here?" Mark said. He'd been thinking about it a while. Again, he got everyone's attention. He was sitting with his legs crossed, in one of the Queen Anne chairs, looking like a philosopher. "If you all hadn't been after Robyn, it wouldn't have played out like it has."

"How do you figure?" JR asked. "You can't mean my sister was supposed to be targeted and possibly shot!" He was offended.

"Hear me out, Dawg," Mark said. "For all intents and purposes, 'Geno' and Sal were our enemies, right?"

They all nodded their heads.

"But look what happened." He patted his chest. "Sal experienced the miracle of a changed heart. He went from trying to harm her, to trying to protect her."

Everyone nodded. "That's true," Eugene agreed. 'The first thing Sal said was, '*we have to go to that young lady's house and make sure Sonny doesn't kill her'."*

Mark nodded. "The team really liked you guys. They came back bragging about how much fun you were, Eugene; *even* Batman. When Sal called out for help, they didn't hesitate to come save you, Eugene. And how is it that it was Ali who decided to take you and Sal home? Arak, you were there, why didn't you?"

"I offered to help Ali, but you're right, Ali was the one who offered to teleport them, first."

Mark kept nodding. "None of us knew Destiny was there. Or that she was his mate." Before anyone could say anything, he said, "Their paths *had* to cross, at that, precise, moment. What would have happened to Destiny's mind, tonight, if Ali hadn't been with her? She'd be insane, for sure." Then he looked at Geno. "You, and your father, were trapped in a lifestyle neither of you chose. You got the opportunity to walk away from that life, with no repercussions. How many people do you know that have been able to do that?" Then he pointed at Nantan. "You got the opportunity to unite with your 'true' family, when you needed *us* the most." Then he shook his head. "Your parents' opinion, of you, doesn't matter, because God finds favor in you. You know how I know?"

Nantan shook his head. "No." He really wanted to believe it, though. He *needed* to believe it. Everyone else wanted to know, too.

"He sent his most powerful Nephilim, to rescue *you*...just before your house blew up! If that ain't favor...then I don't know what is." Then he gazed at everyone in the room. "None of this was happenstance. If you think about it, you can trace it back to when Ditto met Eugene. What are the odds that an, *obviously* straight, 'serious' guy, ended up being, lifelong, best friends, with an, *obviously*, gay, 'clown'; who, by the way, happens to be a hit man, for the mob."

"Hey man!" Eugene protested. "I ain't a clown!"

"Then factor in the odds, that that *'clown'* was in the right place to meet our cousin. And that cousin's sister is mated to one of the team," Mark said. "We have not been left to our own devices; it has all been by design."

They all sat staring at him, speechless.

Nantan held onto his words as though they were the gospel and found peace. He *needed* to know he was in good standing with God.

"Preach Walker," Aden finally said.

~

CHAPTER 10

Destiny woke up still wrapped in Ali's arms. It felt good to be held by him, especially now. Even though she didn't want her parents, and sister, to die, she would rather it be them, instead of her E-du-di. What in the world happened to them? How did a kindhearted family man, like her E-du-di, produce a devil like her father? What would make a man so cold hearted that he didn't hesitate at killing his father, and children? He'd slung that pipe over and over again, with no remorse. Even when he'd hit E-du-di in the head, he hadn't stopped; he just kept beating him. Why was he so angry? He was the one who kicked Nantan out. He was the one who dared him to set foot back on Montana soil.

Her parents had always favored their oldest daughter over their two younger children. She and Nantan were different from them. They had morals. Their parents and sister, on the other hand, were sex addicts...all of them! Their sister was nine years older than them, and was a tramp. But then again, so was their mother. When she and Nantan celebrated their sixteenth birthdays, they'd had one big party. They'd ended up having to call E-du-di to come get them, because their parents had turned their celebration into wild hedonistic parties.

The night her father had beaten Nantan, he'd tried to make her stay. She told him she wouldn't stay anywhere Nantan wasn't welcome. She'd called her E-du-di to come get her. When she'd hung up the phone, her mother slapped her and told her she was an ungrateful, bitch. She wasn't respectful, like Nantan; she'd slapped the hell out of her mother. *"I ain't a little girl and I ain't timid, like Nantan. You keep your, damned, hands off me!"* she'd shouted and went to her bedroom, to pack. Her mother yelled the same thing to her that she'd yelled to Nantan, *"You are not my daughter, you big fat pig!"* Destiny had yelled, right back, *"Thank God! And you, sure as hell, ain't my mother!"*

Her sister had followed her to her room, and attacked her, for hitting *her* mother. *"How dare you hit my mother, you fat cow!"* Her sister was short and small boned, like their mother; neither of them weighed more than one hundred ten pounds. Destiny, on the other hand, was tall, like her father, and had always been stout; weighing, in the area of, one hundred sixty-five pounds.

She'd started packing and didn't acknowledge her sister, because she was used to both women ridiculing her, about her size. The more she ignored her sister, the madder the woman got. Then her sister had made the mistake of pushing her. Destiny hadn't said a word. She'd walked over to the door, locked it and propped a chair underneath the knob.

By the time her E-du-di had arrived she, and her sister, had reached an unspoken agreement. Her sister would never, again, lay a finger on her, and she would never, again, have to beat her sister's ass, for doing it!

That was the last time she'd seen any of them. She'd taken everything she'd wanted that night: her clothing and an Indian quilt her grandmother had made for her. She'd left everything else, including her sister, on the bedroom floor.

She hadn't almost lost her mind over their death; she'd long stopped loving them. It had been the fact that they'd, viciously, beaten her E-du-di, like he was a stranger.

She had no intention of going back to Montana to bury them. They could rot in the sun for all she cared. Her concern was for Nantan and E-du-di. They were carrying a lot of undeserved, guilt.

~

Ali was listening to her thoughts. Since he'd taken her blood, last night, he was able to see her memories, too. He'd almost laughed out loud over the way she'd given her sister a fairly good ass whipping. He heard Destiny's ridiculous warning to her sister, *"I'm gon' beat your ass to death and you'd better not die and I dare you to live!"* Now what kind of sense did that threat make? He almost laughed, again.

But humans were strange. That woman was, at most, five feet four, whereas Destiny was, at least, five feet eight. Destiny outweighed her by, a good, fifty or sixty pounds. What in the world make her think she could whip his "spirit" mate?

Through her memories, he could hear their mother banging and screaming at the door, trying to get in. Her mother was as small as her sister and he wondered if Destiny could have taken them both. Probably. *"You are thinking too much, Darlin,"* Ali whispered to her mind.

She looked up at him. "How did you do that?" She didn't remember what happened last night.

"I had to take your blood last night. It was the only way I could get you out of the darkness. You can talk to me, with your mind too, Destiny."

"I can?"

"You just did, Darlin'." He smiled down at her.

Destiny started squirming and wiggling. He thought she was having another seizer. He sat up. "What's the matter? Are you alright?"

She wiggled, a couple of more times, and then sat up. She pulled the flannel gown over her head and tossed it across the room. "I'm fine, now." She smiled, seductively. Her nipples were erect with desire, longing for his touch; her eyes dark and lustful.

He'd been like Brock, and the others, and given up on casual sex centuries ago. He'd decided last night that he could make love to her and still date her. He must have been crazy thinking one had to negate the other.

Neither of them said a word, as they reached for each other. Ali laid her back down and cast the covers aside. He wanted to see all of her. Of course he'd seen last night, when he'd showered her, how lovely her body was; but he'd deprived himself of truly appreciating her form. It would not have been right, seeing the state of mind she was in. There was nothing to stop him now. She was full figured, and that pleased him. He and the team called each other 'Dawg', but they weren't, and he damn sure didn't want a bone. He ran his hands down the length of her body, kneading and stroking her. He liked the soft, velvety, feel of her flesh. Her voluptuous, breasts reminded him of plump, juicy, caramel apples. He rubbed his thumb across her nipples and observed how they reacted to his touch. He needed to see her body's response to him. He leaned down and suckled her nipples and then rose up and watched them grow. He watched as her breathing became labored. This wasn't voyeurism, because he was a participant. He decided he'd always make love to her in the morning light. Not for his benefit, but hers. So she could see his eyes, as he gazed upon the most perfect creation God had ever formed. He caressed her cheek. *"I've waited for you a long time, Darlin'."* He couldn't stop telling her that. Five thousand years was a long time to wait for the love of your life. He leaned down and kissed her, not like he'd done in the park, but with more passion.

Destiny was mesmerized by the expression on Ali's face. No one had ever looked at her like that before. The way he was *looking* at her was as stimulating as his touch. If it was true that the eyes are the windows to the soul, then it was his soul that desired her. Her body came alive after years of sexual impotence. She'd been sexually active with her ex-fiancée, but she'd never once felt *anything*. It had been a necessary duty for his pleasure, not hers.

But now, Ali was making sure the pleasure was all hers. She ran her hands up and down his hard, masculine back, getting familiar with every ridge. She stroked the dip in his lower back, and caressed his taut cheeks. His skin felt like smooth African leather and made the tips of her fingers quiver, with excitement. *"I wanted to come to you last year, Ali."*

"I've missed you, Destiny," Ali whispered. He was manipulating her flesh like a blind man, reading Braille. Her response to his touch was driving him to go deeper and deeper. She was writhing and moaning and begging him not to stop. He had no intentions of doing that! He didn't need to take her blood, but he would. He wanted her to experience the fullness of being mated with him.

She was reading his mind and she wanted to feel it, too. She wanted to feel everything he had to offer her. *"Do it now, Ali. Let me feel the sensation of our bodies and minds coming together as one."*

Ali's eyes turned red and his canines extended. She held her own breast as he suckled and then pierced it and her womb at the same time. Her womb spasmed and she moaned. If she died this moment, everything would be alright; because she finally knew what nirvana felt like. She held his head to her breast and whispered, *"I love you, Ali! I've been missing you, all my life. Promise you won't ever leave me!"*

Ali braced his elbows on each side of her head, held her face in his hands and stared in her eyes. There it was- that same look. Those eyes were an aphrodisiac. He penetrated her deeper and deeper, faster and faster; he couldn't stop and he couldn't respond. He gazed into those gorgeous eyes and lost himself with visions of their life together.

His eyes were piercing, his gaze unyielding. He didn't respond, but she heard him. With every stroke he was promising her a life filled with love, romance and moments like this. Staring into his eyes, she could see the unspoken promise that their life, together, would not be mundane. Their life, together, would not be limited to hiding behind the estate walls. She caught a glimpse of all the exciting places he would take her; a glimpse of all the things they would do, together. It was liberating to make love with her eyes wide open. To gaze into his eyes and feel his body, connecting to hers; to see his emotional, commitment to her.

She reached up and caressed his, hairy, cheeks. His whiskers were as soft as baby's hair. She ran her thumb along the edge of his slightly opened, lips. He sucked it into his mouth, and seductively, nipped it, never taking his eyes off of her.

Then the strangest thing happened. *Her* canines grew! The Nephilim gene, she'd inherited from Kobabiel, momentarily, came to life. Neither of them questioned it, as she sank her teeth in Ali's left breast. His blood tasted like sweet nectar and it drove her off the cliff.

It was the most erotic thing Ali had ever experienced. He knew for a fact no other Watcher's mate had taken their blood. He didn't have time to analyze it. He threw his head back and exploded.

~

Ali and Destiny lay on their sides facing each other; her leg over his and their bodies still joined. *"How was I able to do that, Ali?"*

"I don't know, but it was the bomb, Darlin'!" He smiled.

She touched her teeth and they were back to

normal. She tried to will her canines into growing again, but couldn't. She leaned over and nibbled his lip, but nothing happened. She tucked her head and suckled his nipple and then bit down...nothing! She had him nibble her thumb, again...nothing!

Ali caressed her breast and started a slow gyration. *"You think too much, Darlin'.*

Destiny's womb clinched and she moaned. *"I could get used to this,"* she whispered, as she gazed into his piercing eyes and watched him, as he made love to her again.

~

The same thing happened. When they reached the height of ecstasy, her canines grew, she pierced his breast and they climaxed.

Theirs was a unique mating!

CHAPTER 11

Ali and Destiny finally made it to the kitchen around eleven; long after breakfast was over. E-du-di and Sal were at the island drinking coffee and talking. Both of them were wondering where they'd gone wrong with their sons.

"E-du-di," Destiny said, and walked over, and hugged him. "How are you this morning?"

"I'm well, child. How are you?" He was examining her face, for signs of distress. Her reaction to her parent's death was a concern to him. He had worried about her all night. Sal had wanted to go and sit in the gazebo, but he'd refused to leave until he saw for himself that she was okay.

He knew everyone saw the motivation behind him killing his son; but he wouldn't have let them lay a finger on Destiny or Nantan, either. Not to mention Kwanita. Those three grandchildren were his children. He'd stepped up and taken care of them when their parent's couldn't...or wouldn't.

"I'm okay," Destiny answered and then

looked around the room. "Where is Nantan?"

"He's out with the rest of the men working on the development. The physical labor will be good for him. Ditto wants you to start on the permits, as soon as possible."

"I lost my computer when Nantan's house blew up."

"I thought you kept most of your information on one of those little things. What did you call it?"

"Thumb drive. But it was in my purse. We lost everything, E-du-di."

"I have a laptop that I never use," Ali informed her. "Will that help to get you started?"

"Yeah, it will. I have to rebuild my files. I'll need Nantan to help me, though. He built the application I use."

"Well let's wait until they come in for lunch. In the meantime, Sal, I need to get you guys some clothes," Ali said.

"That's kind of you, but I can afford to buy my own clothes. If I can use the computer I can order everything. I know that Brocks doesn't want us leaving the estate."

Brock walked in the kitchen carrying

Elizabeth. "Why do you need to leave the estate?" He frowned.

"I don't. I was just telling Ali I can order us some clothes, online."

"Oh yeah, I forgot you'd lost everything. Have Chef order everything you need. He has the account number."

"I have my own account."

"If there is any activity in your account your enemies will know that you didn't die in that house," E-du-di warned him.

Sal smiled. "The majority of my disposable funds are in an account in Nantan's name. I always planned on, one day, leaving that life."

"Did Antonio know about that account?" Ali asked, remembering that Antonio was the one who told everyone where Geno lived.

"No. No one knew but Geno. I never trusted my son." Then he frowned. "He died never knowing that Geno was his brother."

"You never told him?" Ali frowned.

"No. My son, like Hania's, was petty and vindictive. If he'd thought, for a moment, that Geno was next in line to inherit the business, he would have tried to kill him years ago."

Hania nodded his head. He and Sal had a lot in common. They were developing a bond based on regret and grief. "That was my son, too, hateful to the bone," he said and looked at Destiny. "I'm sorry, Child."

"You don't have anything to apologize for, E-du-di. Both my parents were evil. I've always known that. But my mother was the worse. She could persuade my father to do anything. I swear most of my life I never believed she was my mother. I am nothing like her. I have never had anything in common with her. The day I left she screamed at me that I was not her daughter. Just like she told Nantan he wasn't her son, when they threw him out. When she said that, to me, my heart leaped with joy."

~

Ali caught the way Brock and Hania looked at each other. It was just a brief look, but it'd been enough to peak his interest. He wondered if there was any truth to Destiny's mother's statement. If so, then who was her mother? And where was she? When he'd looked into Destiny's memories, he'd noticed the stark difference between her and her mother and sister. It was no doubt her father was her father, she looked like Hania. But, he remembered her thinking about her parents being sexual degenerates. Maybe her father had gotten some woman pregnant and kept the child. She would have still been his third child, which made her eligible to be his 'spirit' mate. When he got her alone he'd look at her memories again. He could travel back as far as the womb for memories she would've been too young to remember.

He was busy wondering what he would discover and how he would handle the information he'd glean from her mind, and didn't realize Brock had noticed his behavior.

~

Brock had been around Ali long enough to know when his analytical mind was churning. As a rule he never violated his team member's private thoughts, but Ali hadn't responded to Destiny's questions. For him to ignore his mate he had to be deep in thought about something important. He eased into Ali's mind. Damn, this was bad. He didn't realize he and Hania had been caught glancing at each other. He had the ability to corner off his thoughts but still maintain a link to his team. So even though Ali saw them, he didn't know what was on Brock's mind. Brock was glad that Ali didn't try to listen to Hania's thoughts. It was considered rude to do so.

But now, Ali was going to open a door that, once opened, would fall off its hinges. There would be no closing it, again. Destiny had come close to losing her mind last night. He had no doubt this information would destroy her, and in turn, Ali. He wasn't about to let that happen. *"Seek and you will not like what you find, Ali."*

~

Ali was lost in thought and was caught off guard when Brock spoke to him. He actually jumped. Then he saw the expression on Brock's face and knew the truth. Destiny's mother was not her mother. And her real mother hadn't given her away, either. Something awful had happened to the woman. Seeing how vicious Destiny's parents had been to Hania, he didn't put anything past them. His heart leaped...they'd killed her! *"Nawl, Brock! Nawl man! Oh damn, tell me it's not what I'm thinking!"*

"Some mysteries are best left unsolved. You have your mate and you both are happy, let that be enough. For the sake of your mate, leave it be."

"Man you know me. I gotta know."

"If you pursue this line of investigation, it will have a ricochet effect throughout the entire estate. This family experienced a devastating blow, last night. None of them can handle another one, Dawg."

~

Destiny hit Ali. "Hey, what are you thinking about?" she asked.

"I'm sorry, Darlin'. I was thinking about where I was taking you tonight," he lied, with a smile.

"We won't be going anywhere if I don't get these permits going. The guys have already broken the law by pouring the foundations without them."

"Okay, I'll get the laptop," Ali said, and walked away. He needed to get away from her, for a minute. He would have staked his life on the promise that he would never lie to her. But he just did and it didn't sit well with his conscience. In the end, Brock was right, he *shouldn't* search for answers.

He *really* shouldn't...

~

Destiny sat the laptop up in the dining room. Brock told her she could take one of the empty bedrooms and turn it into her office. She agreed, but she needed to get busy now and would do it later. She had her cousin, Faith, download and send previous forms to her email address. Those forms had telephone numbers and internet links that she'd need to access. She and Faith worked closely together on every construction project their cousins worked on. Faith also sent her copies of the blueprints. They were awesome. This community was going to look like a mini Hollywood. She'd have to get them recorded at the county office. Hopefully, she'd be finished in time, today, to have a carrier pick them up and deliver them. Thankfully, she was also the appraiser so no outsiders would have to set foot on the property.

~

Ali left Destiny alone, because she was engrossed in her work. He decided to put on some jeans and go help with the buildings. He needed to distract his mind with productive, physical, labor. Otherwise he was going to think himself, into doing what he knew he shouldn't do.

CHAPTER 12

On his way back to their room Ali ran into Lara. She saw how distracted he was, and was concerned. "Ali?"

"Hey, Lara," Ali said offhandedly.

"Something's wrong." It was a statement. She thought it had to do with what had happened last night. Maybe Destiny was in bad shape.

Ali tried but he couldn't lie. Lara and James were his best friends. "Do you have a minute?"

"Yeah, come on back to my suite." She reached for his hand. They were clammy. Yeah, something was wrong with her friend.

"Where is James?"

"He and Deuce are out working with the guys."

Good. He didn't want to discuss this with everyone. He and James were best friends, but Lara was the one whose ear he trusted above all others.

~

When they made it to her suite, Lara and Ali

sat at the small, butcher block, table. "Is Destiny alright this morning?" she asked, with a concerned look on her face. The girl had almost lost her mind last night. Lara's imagination went into overdrive. She envisioned her cousin, in her room, catatonic. That would be awful!

"Yeah she's fine. She's working in the dining room, right now, on paperwork for the site," Ali answered, staring down at his hands. Maybe Brock was right. This was a Pandora's Box. But he needed to confide in someone. He didn't trust anyone, but Lara. Especially after finding out that she'd known about James' heritage, all along, and never told a soul. James and his boys never told the secret either, but it was their secret. Lara kept James' secret even before she knew they'd marry and have children. That's what he liked most about her...she could keep *someone else's* secret.

"Talk to me, Ali. You know how dear you are to me. I hate seeing you so distraught." She reached for his hand. "What's the matter, Honey?"

"You can never tell this to anyone, Lara. Not even James," Ali said and squeezed her hand. "Promise me."

This had to be, *really,* serious for him not to want James to know. He and James shared everything. She was almost tempted to say she didn't want to know. But she was compelled to help her friend. "Alright, I promise."

"I don't think your aunt was Destiny's mother," he said, flat out, staring Lara in the eye.

~

Ali wasn't expecting the look Lara gave him. It wasn't one of shock or inquiry. It was without a doubt…confirmation. "Oh God, you knew!"

She nodded her head. "I've always known. But no one else does," she said sadly.

"What happened, Lara?"

"It would kill everyone in my family if they knew, Ali."

"I've gotta know, Lara. It is weighing heavy on my mind. Is her mother still alive?" he asked, even though he knew the answer.

Lara looked down at her hands and shook her head. "I was, only, nine years old."

"Nine!" Ali asked; or maybe just stated. What a terrible burden for a little girl to have to shoulder.

Lara nodded her head. "I'd gone to Montana, to stay with them, for summer vacation. Their oldest daughter, Seke, and I were the same age. We were very close, at the time. We did everything together. One summer I'd go there, for two weeks. The next summer she'd come here, for two weeks."

Ali could tell by her expression she was in the territory of fond memories. He didn't want to rush her because her memories would only get worse. That much he was sure of. "Amanda and Jodi didn't go?"

"Amanda was seven, Jodi was five. At that age big sisters want time away from their little sisters, you know. Mama and Daddy were always good to allow me to be away from them for two weeks out of the year. The rest of the year they followed me like my shadow. I played games that were too young for me to be playing, because they liked them. If we were watching television, one would sit on each side of me and hold my hand. I read to them every night before they went to sleep. If it was storming outside they'd both crawl in the bed with me, because they were afraid."

"You were their hero, Lara." Ali smiled.

"Now when I look back they weren't so bad, after all." She nodded. "I was a good big sister. But I just needed time to be a kid, myself."

"You still are a good big sister, Lara." Ali smiled. "Even to me."

"There was a wooded area, behind my Uncle's house. Seke and I used to play hide and seek out there." She smiled at the memory. "One day we saw her parents strike out walking down the path and decided to follow them."

"They didn't know you were behind them?" Ali asked.

"No. We were playing hide and seek with them, they just didn't know it. They never once looked back or they would have seen us, for sure."

"So what happened?" He decided to push.

"They knocked on the back door of this woman's house. The minute she opened the door she started shouting at them, *"You can't have my baby!"* She tried to close the door, but my uncle pushed it in. He and my aunt went in, but left the door open. Seke, and I, snuck inside to see what was going on."

"They still didn't see you?"

"No. They were too busy. My aunt grabbed the baby. My uncle put his hand over the woman's mouth to keep her from screaming. Then he picked her up and carried her into the bathroom." She paused and looked at Ali. "We didn't see it, but we heard the water running. We could hear her fighting him. He drowned her in the bathtub, Ali. Seke and I ran back into the woods. We were afraid they'd kill us next. We hid until we saw them leave with the baby."

Ali was holding both of his hands over his mouth. He was shaking his head. Brock was right; he didn't like what he was hearing. If Destiny ever knew the truth this would, no doubt, destroy her. He doubted he'd be able to bring her back from her dark place if she knew.

He wanted to kill those bastards, all over again. What kind of woman stays with a man who would do something like that? It wasn't an accident; it was coldblooded and calculated. But, then again, she had to be, too. After all she was in on it. And poor Lara had been just a child. He wondered if seeing that tragedy had fashioned her life. Was that why she became a marksman? So she could protect her children, even from James. He looked at her and frowned. "They drowned Destiny's mother!"

~

Nothing on heaven or earth could have prepared Ali for what Lara said next. "The baby was Nantan, Ali."

Ali jumped up so fast he knocked the chair over. "Nantan!" he shouted. "Oh my God, Lara! They drowned her while she was still carrying Destiny!" He knew there was only seven months difference in their ages. His eyes turned red. His rage was growing at an alarming rate and he wanted to tear this room apart.

Lara stood up, sat Ali's chair back upright and then forced him to sit down. She grabbed his hands and, again, he was not ready for what she said next. "Nantan and Destiny didn't have the same mother."

"What!"

"When they left with Nantan we waited a minute and followed them. Seke and I were holding hands, because we were afraid. We thought they were going home and would realize we weren't there. But they didn't."

Ali had never before felt such a sense of dread. He'd opened this can of worms and now he had to see it through. "Where did they go?"

"The path had a fork in it that veered off in another direction. It was a lot more wooded, than the first, so we were able to hide a little better; although it didn't matter, because neither of them ever looked back. The lady was sitting in a chair in her back yard. When she saw them coming she tried to get up, but her stomach was real big and she couldn't move fast enough."

"She was pregnant!" Ali asked.

"Yes. I didn't know that's what it was, until later."

"With Destiny?" Ali's voice cracked.

Lara nodded her head. "My uncle grabbed her and stuffed a lot of pills down her throat. He held her mouth and nose until she was forced to swallow them. He waited, for what seemed like forever, until she'd passed out. Then he went inside the house and came back out with a telephone up to his ear."

"Who did he call?"

"His friend. He was one of the medicine men on the reservation. He came over and they took the baby out of the woman by c-section. I didn't know what that was at the time. It just seemed to me and Seke that they'd gutted her. The woman died."

Ali was shaking like a leaf. God if he could turn back the hands of time he'd never take this journey of discovery. "Destiny."

"Yes. While they were cleaning up their mess, Seke and I ran back to their house." Lara looked at Ali, with tears in her eyes. "We were just little kids, we didn't mean to see."

"How did they explain the babies to their neighbors?"

"They moved to a different reservation, that day. They had it already planned out. Being a child it didn't registered that they didn't have much furniture in the house. We were sleeping on pallets on the floor. Seke had very little clothing, because they were all at the new location."

"Hania didn't question it?"

"E-du-di lived a long ways away from them, on a different reservation. He and my uncle didn't get along and he hadn't seen them in almost two years. But when they moved they moved to the reservation that E-du-di was living on. He accepted his son and his family right off. He had no idea what happened."

"You didn't tell your parents?"

"I was afraid. I told no one. When we got to their new home I told E-du-di I wanted to go home, right then. He could tell how upset I was, but I wouldn't tell him what was wrong. He called my parents and told them he was bringing me home."

Ali was trying not to push Lara. He could tell the memories still frightened her. But there were gaps, in her recounting, that needed to be filled. "How did you get to Montana, Lara?"

"Daddy and my uncle always split the distance and met up at the same rest stop, along the highway. That way both could get back home in the same day."

"That's why they didn't questions the two new babies. They would have never seen that your aunt hadn't ever been pregnant."

Lara nodded her head. "Mama would visit E-du-di, but I don't believe she saw my uncle during those visits."

"So did you ever go back?"

"No. I think that was when my cousin lost her mind. She came the next summer, but she was different. When I tried to ask her about it she pretended she didn't know what I was talking about. She called me a big fat liar. Now I realize that she'd hid that trauma so deep in her mind she really didn't remember, Ali. After that she didn't like me anymore. And I, sure as hell, was never going to that place again."

"Why didn't you tell somebody…anybody?"

"I was a child. I was afraid they'd gut my mother and take me and my sisters."

"You didn't think H could protect you?" From what he knew about the man, he'd kill Satan, himself, to protect his family.

"I didn't want to lose my father, either. I didn't have a name for the things my uncle and aunt were into, until years later. But they both delved into the occult. They followed the Diana doctrine of shameless rituals of prostitution and the mutilation of humans for sacrifice."

"Diana!" She was a vile false goddess of

virginity and motherhood, which was ridiculous. That ancient civilization of Ephesus had set themselves up to be possessed by demons. He hadn't heard of anybody still believing in, or practicing, that crap in centuries. "So is it safe to say that Destiny's and Nantan's mothers weren't the only women they killed?"

"That would be my guess. Look at how they came at E-du-di. After seeing that, you know they had to have killed before, as a group. Remember how they strategically moved so E-du-di wouldn't be able to keep an eye on all three at the same time? That was planned, Ali."

Ali nodded, remembering what her aunt had said. "Nantan has to be sacrificed."

"Yes!" Lara nodded. "I've always feared they'd get in their minds to kill me, because I knew the truth."

"They never said anything to you about where the babies came from?"

"No. They figured we were just kids and maybe thought the babies had been with friends while they were in the process of moving."

That made sense. With no furniture or baby

beds the babies could have been at someone else's house until they got ready to leave for their new home.

~

Ali and Lara sat staring at each other for a long while; both of them thinking the same thing. They'd just forged a bond tighter than anyone would ever know. This would be their secret. And they'd take it to their grave...if they were to have one.

"Thank you, Ali," Lara finally said.

"For what! For making you relive what had to be the most horrific event a child has ever experienced?" He was disgusted with himself. "I'm sorry I did that to you, Lara."

"No. Thank you for being my sounding board." She smiled. "I hadn't thought about what I'd seen in years. Then last night it all came rushing back and I had no one I could talk to about it. How did you know, anyway?"

"Destiny said she's always suspected that her mother wasn't her mother. That got me to thinking about how different they were in size and disposition."

"She and Nantan can't ever know the truth." Lara frowned.

Ali nodded. "It would destroy my mate; and Nantan, too."

"But can't Destiny hear your thoughts?"

"Only the ones I allow her to hear. I didn't think I'd ever hold anything back from my 'spirit' mate once I found her. But I can't ever let her know what happened to her real mother."

"I agree."

"How did you deal with this, Lara? All by yourself?" Ali was about to burst. He was holding his temper, but he wanted to kill somebody, for what had happened to Destiny's mother. He needed to get himself under control or Destiny would sense something was wrong. He could lie to her by omission, but he wasn't sure he could look in her face and lie, again.

"I never forgot, but I blocked it out of my mind."

"I always tease you about being mean, but you know you really are not, right."

She smiled. "You say that because I'm going to let you be my daughter's Godfather."

"Yeah, that too." He smiled, but it didn't reach his eyes. He was angry for Destiny and Nantan; and he was angry for Lara. He was even angry that their father had destroyed their other daughter's sanity, as well. His temples jumped, as he fought to force his rage back down. He didn't want to scare Lara further, but he was teetering. "But there's a difference in being mean and being guarded."

"The minute I found out I was pregnant I was determined to learn how to shoot. I pushed James to the brink some days, but I was determined to protect myself, and my children. No one was ever going to steal my babies. That's why I fought so hard for Sam when they tried to take his daughters away from him."

Ali nodded. James had told him how she'd gone off on the judge. He'd said Lara had been ready to rumble if the court decided Sam couldn't keep his children. Now he understood why. She'd seen those babies stolen from their mothers. He understood her a lot more, now.

~

So what, call him nosey, if you will, but

Brock knew Ali wouldn't let it go. Honestly, he wouldn't have either. He was sitting quietly in the conference room listening to Lara tell the tale. To hear Lara recounting the event was heartbreaking. At some points in the conversation her voice sounded like a frightened little child.

He'd seen it all in Hania's mind, anyway. Hania had gotten a glimpse of what happened when Lara had been so adamant to go home. He knew something had happened, but she was too frightened to say. Hania couldn't prove they'd done it, because he hadn't seen it. Mixed with the fact that he loved his son and despised his daughter-in-law, he was in a precarious position. His daughter-in-law had done nothing, but watch. She could claim she was afraid and get off scout free. With both babies no longer having their natural mothers he wasn't about to leave them in the hands of that, she devil, faux one.

Hania had however, confronted his son. He promised him as long as the babies were treated right, he could live free. But the minute he saw anything bad happening to his grandchildren he'd turn him in. His son had accepted the agreement saying he loved his children. And he'd been good to them until the night he found out Nantan was gay. But too much time had passed and it would hurt his grandchildren to learn that he'd kept that secret from them all these years.

~

Lara was Brock's favorite sister-in-law and he wanted to do something. He did what Ali couldn't do. He traveled through her memories and saw the tragedy, as it unfolded. Those two little girls were terrified. By the time they got to Destiny's mother's house, Seke had soiled her pants. Lara was holding her hand over Seke's mouth, trying to keep her from screaming. Seke's legs froze and she couldn't move on her on. Lara grabbed her by the arm and dragged her, as she ran back to her uncle's house. Seke couldn't be blamed for her actions, against Hania; she'd lost her mind, that day in the woods.

Then another scene caught Brock's eye. He tilted his head sideways and squinted. "Um, Imagine that!" he said to himself.

~

"I warned you not to do this!" Brock said.

"When you leave Lara, come to the conference room, Ali."

Ali could tell, by the sternness of his voice, that Brock was not happy with him. He cursed. "Damn!"

"What?" Lara asked.

"Do NOT tell her!" Brock warned. *"She does not need to know that I am aware of this situation."*

"Nothing. This is just a mess," Ali lied. When was he ever going to learn that Brock was nosey, as Hell?"

"Don't worry about how nosey I am; you just get your butt in here."

"I need to go, Lara. Are you going to be okay, by yourself?"

"I'm good. I was getting ready to go get Sylvia and Sheila anyway."

CHAPTER 13

Ali swaggered down the hall, towards the conference room, with his head up and shoulders squared...defensively. Brock was fixin' to chew on his backside for digging into Destiny's family history. If Brock wanted to denigrate him for it, it was a fight he was willing to have. Brock was their leader, and he respected the hell out of him, but he was stepping out of bounds. Destiny was *his* woman and it was his duty, no it was his right, to find out everything about her. Her father had, egregiously, deprived her of her mother and there wasn't a damn thing he could do about it. And although he wished he'd never trampled down this path, the dust was stirred now. And he was prepared to tell Brock to, back the hell off, and mind his own damn business!

"I believe you just did," Brock said.

Ali slowed down. *"Shit!"* A man couldn't even think these days, without that bastard hearing his private thoughts. What the hell ever happened to respect and privacy!   And how was Brock hearing his thoughts, anyway? He knew damn well he'd closed the link. Brock was *too* damn nosey.

"I heard that, too!" Brock taunted him.

"Good!   Next you'll be spying on my morning constitutionals!" Ali snapped at him.

"How do you know I don't already?" Brock kept taunting him.

Ali was an, intimidating, six and a half feet tall, two hundred sixty five pounds, hunk of, solid, muscles. Although he could cripple his opponent by attacking their gastro system; he was as fierce a fighter as the rest of the team. He wasn't afraid of Brock, or Seraphiel, for that matter!

"You should be!" Brock said, dryly.

"Get the hell out of my head, man!" Ali yelled at him, then stopped and hit the wall. *"What the hell is wrong with you? You are pissing me off!"*

"Why did you stop? Did you realize you just might be afraid, after all?" Brock asked. Brock knew Ali was furious, because he wasn't thinking clearly.   Why didn't he just teleport to the conference room, instead of walking? That was a

long walk to take, if you didn't have to. *"Is it possible your thoughts have picked a fight that your ass can't win?"*

"Don't push me, Brock. I know how powerful you are, but don't try me!" Ali shouted. *"Not now!"* Even though he was speaking with his mind; his African accent, still deepened and resonated the level of his irritation.

"Only thing being tried is my patience. What is taking you so long? Get your butt in here, now, Ali! Brock shouted.

Ali huffed and tried to calm himself down. Brock had worked his last nerve and he was prepared to go the distance. If Brock thought he could intimidate him, well he'd better think again. He was being intrusive, rude and inconsiderate. Too many people, humans at that, were in this house for them to have an all out fight. But if Brock brought it, then it was on.

"You are not thinking clearly, Ali. You know I don't have to lift a finger, to bring it! I can reach out and 'bitch' slap you from anywhere! You know that." Brock kept pushing. *"Now stop stalling and get your ass in here!"*

Ali was a man on a mission. He stretched his, bowed, legs maximizing ground coverage. His shoulders rolled and his arms, angrily, swung in rhythm with the rapidity of his stride. The echoes from his feet, forcefully, pounding the floor, sent out a warning signal to the estate's residents…'get the *hell* out of my way'.

He passed Amanda and Jodi in the hall, but did not acknowledge them. They, smartly, jumped to the side, as he stormed by. He'd had enough of Brock! Now he identified with all the other members who'd wanted a piece of Brock's hide. He wondered if Brock had Ram, on standby, to protect him this time, too.

"Now I know you're trippin'. I don't need Ram to protect me from anyone and certainly not from you!" Brock kept messing with him. *"I suggest you rethink your attitude and actions before you get more than your feelings hurt, boy!"*

"Have it your way you, nosey ass, bastard!" Ali was so angry he was now, practically, running towards the conference room. His legs bending at the knee, with each step, were overly accentuated the bow in them. He took the stairs three at a time

and the floor tiles were, literally, creaking under the pressure of his, angered, feet. With momentum at his tail, he damaged the corner of a protruding wall, as he made the final turn in the basement.

This was the end of the road; there would be no turning back from here on out. Brock had pushed him too far. Brock's demeaning words hadn't created a fracture, but a break in Ali's trust. The nerve of him, talking about 'bitch' slapping him! Bitch Slapping!

Brock kept antagonizing him. *"Boy, not only will I 'bitch' slap you; I will tap that ass, if you don't get in here!"* Brock shouted and said, *"Don't force me to come get you, Ali!"*

~

Ali's eyes were smoldering with red, and amber, fury. He may not be able to whip Brock's ass, but he wasn't a punk either! Brock could try that crap on him that he'd done to Ram, if he wanted to. But if he tossed him into Hell, there would be no turning back. He wouldn't forgive or ever forget. Michael would have to put him on another team, because there would never again, be any peace in the estate.

~

He burst through the conference room door, ready for a knockdown. "WHAT THE HELL IS *WRONG* WITH YOU, BROCK?" he shouted, and then stopped dead in his tracks. The entire team was seated at the conference table. They were all staring at him wondering what the hell was wrong with *him*!

"Have a seat, Ali," Brock said calmly. His demeanor was not confrontational, but conciliatory. He didn't look like he was aiming for a fight; or to do bodily harm to Ali. Even his eyes were compassionate. *"I feel ya, Dawg."*

Ali's heart was racing. He stood there confused as hell. Then it hit him what Brock had done. He'd been so angry at Brock's spying on him he'd forgotten he was enraged over Destiny's mother's death. If he had ran into Destiny in the hall, after hearing what had happened; he would not have been able to keep from telling her, just like he'd told Lara. And he *had* passed Amanda and Jodi in the hall, but they'd just moved to the side and let him pass. Thanks to Brock he'd been too angry to say hello to them; let alone reveal the family secret.

~

Brock hadn't called Ali to come to the conference room to reprimand him; he'd never do that with the team looking on. He'd taken all of Ali's insubordinate and insolent words, yet he wasn't offended. It was his plan all along, to take the brunt of Ali's rage on his shoulders, so he wouldn't speak to anyone else about Destiny's tragic birth. And Ali would have too, had it not been for Brock screwing with his head.

~

Ali had to work hard to get his emotions under control. Whereas, he'd come ready to fight and sever all ties, he now wanted to thank Brock. Just like those 'Principle' demons had done, Brock had manipulated the hell out of his emotions, but he'd done it for a *righteous* cause. Neither of them wanted their mates to suffer another emotional trauma, like they had, last night. Ali, finally, sat down and shook his head. He looked, regretfully, at Brock. He'd said some terrible things. *"Man, I didn't realize..."*

Brock cut him off. *"We are a team. Even*

when it doesn't seem like it, I'll always have your back, Dawg." Then he laughed. *"But you are out of your mind if you think I'd want to witness your morning constitutional!"*

Ali laughed out loud. That *was* gross. Hell he didn't even want to witness it. But he still felt bad for the things he'd said to Brock.

He noticed none of the Walkers were seated at the table. It was just the Watchers, including Satariel...and Kobabiel! This could only mean one thing. They were going into battle! But with whom?

~

"Listen," Brock started. "I told you, you should not venture down this path. But now that you have we have some business to handle."

"What path?" Chaz asked. Brock had not clued any of them in on what was happening. He'd simply informed them that they needed to come to a private meeting, immediately. And that the Walkers were not invited.

"What are you talking about? They are all dead. There is no one for me to exact retribution on!" Ali said sharply. Now his anger was back where it was, before Brock accosted his mind.

"Who's all dead?" Batman asked. Brock and Ali were both speaking french. Well not even french, because they, all, understood that language. If they were talking about Destiny's parents, was Brock planning on bringing them back? He wouldn't mind, if he did. Although they had not threatened Robyn directly, the mere fact that they'd planned on coming to the estate was threat enough. He knew everyone at the table felt the same way. They'd all discussed the possibility of Brock bringing them back.

~

Brock ignored both Chaz and Batman. He shook his head. "Not all."

Ali raised his eyebrows and sat straight up. "What do you mean, not all? Who else is there? Is Destiny still in danger?" His voice squeaked.

All the other members sat up straight, too. Were there more than just those three who knew about the plan and wanted to kill their mates?

"Who else is there, Brock?" Doc finally asked. His eyes were pinkish…moving towards the red zone. "Is Brighteyes still in danger?"

~

Brock leaned back in his chair, opened his mind and allowed them to see, for themselves. He knew it would have the same effect on his team that it had had on him. He knew their minds would go to the same dark place his had gone.

~

All the members, including Satariel and Kobabiel, leaned forward and placed their elbows on the table. Their fingers were pressed against their mouths, with their chins resting on their palms. It appeared, as though, their hands were holding their mouths closed as gruesome scenes began to unfold. Scenes of one woman, after another, being mutilated, as their babies were being cut out of them. Then the women were placed on an altar and ritually sacrificed, as they bled to death. None of them had to ask who those first two babies were.

~

"This *can't* be just a coincidence," Ali finally squeaked.

"The ritual is part of the "Diana" cult's practices. Many women have gone missing, in

Montana, since Destiny's birth. The majority can be attributed to this man. He's, nothing short of, a serial killer," Brock replied.

None of them knew much about the "Diana" occult, but it appeared to be fashioned after their lives. It reminded each of them, what they'd done to their own mothers, from the inside out. Hadn't their mothers been sacrificed, so that they could live? This was personal, and they were, *all*, psyched for battle.

"I presume Hezekiah and his boys were not aware of this travesty?" Doc asked.

"No. They never knew," Ali replied. "Only Lara, and she never told anyone."

"I didn't think so. Knowing what we know about Hezekiah and Elijah they never would have sat back, all these years, knowing what happened to Nantan's and Destiny's mothers," Doc agreed. "Nor would H have let his daughter experience this trauma without seeking blood!"

"Not to mention Howard and Luther would have gone 'shade', without government sanction, and wiped this entire occult out of existence," Chaz added. He knew his father-in-law would never have gone along with this disgrace.

"I agree," Batman said. "Dad would not have let this slide."

"It was a wise decision not to let the Walkers in on this meeting, Brock," Dan said, shaking his head.

"This is Watcher business!" Chaz said. "This act disparages the memories of *our* mothers!"

~

Then it struck Ali what he'd just seen. "Wait a minute! That bastard is still alive!" He'd been focused on what they'd done to Destiny's mother and all the other women; he'd failed to zone in on the 'so called' doctor. "He's still *alive*, Brock?"

Brock slowly, and purposefully, nodded his head. "And he's still at it." Then he said, "I was wrong, Ali. If you had followed my advice, and not questioned Lara, we never would've known he was still killing innocent women."

There wasn't a phrase coined that could adequately depict what Ali was feeling. He'd known, all along, that Brock didn't have an ego; but for him to admit he was wrong, in front of the entire room, heartened him. He'd come in the conference room ready to sever all ties, with the best man he'd ever known. Under normal circumstances he would've been able to analyze what Brock was doing to him. But these were not normal circumstances. He wished he could undo all the negative things he'd thought about Brock.

Ali shook his head. "I could not see what you could, Brock. If you had not been watching and listening, I would have only gotten half the information. I'm sorry for doubting your motives. Everything you did was for the sanity of me and *my* mate. I owe you a debt of gratitude for that, man. I was wrong for calling you a 'nosey' ass bastard."

"You called him a 'nosey' ass bastard?" Ram asked and he and the other members started laughing.

Ali and Brock, both, ignored Ram. Brock knew he'd pushed Ali to the brink of walking away, but he'd had no choice. All the residents of the estate had been through enough last night, including Ali. He couldn't, no he wouldn't allow that to happen again, at least not today. The minute Ali had been stopped by Lara; Brock had known what he had to do. If anyone else had stopped Ali, he would have done the same thing. Ali hadn't even been thinking clearly enough to *remember* he could have just teleported to the conference room.

Brock also knew that Ali really believed that he would physical harm him. He needed to rectify that. Watchers, and demons, around the world always remembered who he used to be. "We are all members of one body, Ali. Each of us have been imbued with our, own, special gifts. Not to use against one another, but together; to make this body, strong. But, as your leader, it is incumbent on me to carrying the loads that are too heavy for you guys to bear. As your leader, I am charged with knowing when to intervene, on *your* behalf. It doesn't make me greater, or more important, than, any of you. On the contrary, out of all of us, I am the least. I know my worth and I know your worth... *to me*. That's why we are one of the most powerful teams, Dawg; because, as your leader, I *know* your worth."

Brock paused and looked at Ram. "I was wrong, three thousand years ago, when I tossed you in Hell. I compounded that wrong, by leaving you there for thirty days. I not only hurt you but I hurt my reputation, as well. I don't give a damn what others think of me, but I value the opinion of my inner circle. I can't live with the knowledge that each of you, honestly, believe I will hurt you. For the record, I will never, again, do that to you or, any of my brothers. Nor will I ever do, any of you, emotional, or physical, harm." Then he looked around the table, at his team and then back at Ali. He shook his head. "And I, most certainly, will never allow any of you to leave this team, or your home, Ali. Ever! Together we will stand and I'll be *damned* if we fall!"

Ali and Brock stood up and reached for each other's forearm. Then they gave each other a one armed hug, solidifying the promise Brock had just made to all of them.

~

The team didn't know what had happened between Brock and Ali. But whatever it was it had affected them both, greatly. Everyone surmised that just like when they'd found their mates and wanted to attack Brock, Ali had been consumed by that same, mutinous, spirit. And just like with them, Brock had looked beyond Ali's treacherous behavior and understood his need. He may think he was the least, but they knew better. Brock was the foundation…the corner stone that held their team together. And now he'd poured out his soul, to them. They were all moved, beyond words, by his decree. Together, they all stood and faced their leader. Then, one by one, they placed their right hands over their hearts and pledged, "Semper Fidelis! Always Faithful! Always Loyal!"

Brock slightly bowed his head to them. They felt him mentally place his hand over theirs.

~

Kobabiel sat, quietly, listening to Seraphiel's statement to his team. That was some touching stuff, there. Seraphiel had come a long way from the man he'd once known. In the past he would have spouted his egotistical, *'my word is law',* crap. Then he would have, forcefully, snatched Ali into the conference room and jacked him for disobeying *'his'* word!' Now his demeanor was one of humility and servitude.

Like Seraphiel, Kobabiel had exceptional powers and could penetrate any link. He'd heard

Seraphiel antagonizing Ali and knew why he'd done it. After hearing the details of his mate's mother's death, Ali was struggling to keep control of his rage. He'd forgotten everything Kobabiel had taught him, about self control and examination. He'd even forgotten he could teleport. It was, tactically, brilliant the way Seraphiel had made himself the conduit for Ali's anger. He'd methodically taken control of Ali's madness and aimed it at himself. But, Seraphiel hadn't taken Ali's words to heart. He'd known Ali was under emotional duress, and that his words were nothing more than sounding brass.

Kobabiel searched all of the men's memories and saw how Seraphiel had interacted with them, during their, individual, crises. Seraphiel had handled all of them in a like manner when they'd found their mates. He was, especially, impressed with how Seraphiel had handled Chaziel's breakdown. He almost laughed, out loud, at how Seraphiel handled Batariel, Denel and Chaziel when they'd all wanted the same retribution. Kobabiel's head bounced from side to side as he mimicked Seraphiel in his mind, *'I am Seraphiel!*

My word is Law!' Kobabiel thought to himself... *Yada! Yada!*

But Seraphiel had an uncanny knack for meeting each of their needs when they needed him the most. Seraphiel had, finally, learned that a leader's role wasn't to yoke those under his leadership. But rather, a leader's role is to prop them up on their leaning side; so that they can stand up straight and perform their duties, with pride and dignity.

Kobabiel wished he could take all the credit for Seraphiel's transformation, but he could not. He'd led Seraphiel to the fountain of empathy; but Seraphiel had drunk of it, on his own accord. Seraphiel had grown, in the last couple of centuries, and Kobabiel's cup was running over with pride for his friend.

CHAPTER 14

Satariel had only vaguely heard what was going on between Brock and his men. He'd been preoccupied with what he'd just seen. "We can never tell our 'spirit' mates," he almost whispered. Everyone turned to look at him. He had a peculiar expression on his face. His voice was full of grief! "Sarah would not be able to deal with this." He took a deep breath and looked at Ali. "The branches on my tree stretch far and wide." They, *all*, could see how distressed he was.

Ali felt sorrow for Satariel. "Were they your grandchildren?"

Satariel nodded his head. "They were my granddaughters."

That was shocking to hear. "Did you know what happened to them?" Kobabiel asked. "Did you know my grandson killed your granddaughters?"

"No!" Satariel said sharply, then realized he sounded curt. "I'm sorry, my friend. This is not your fault. Besides, he was *our* grandson, yours and mine."

Kobabiel nodded. "That is very true."

"Were they the third sibling, in their families?" Brock asked.

Everyone knew why he'd asked.

Satariel shook his head. "No. First and second child; they were sisters."

"Sisters?" Brock frowned.

"Yeah, but that didn't mean they couldn't have been a 'spirit' mate. Sarah was the oldest and she is mine," Satariel added.

"How?" Chaz asked.

"All 'spirit' mates aren't third sibling. Just those in your group have been. Everyone on my team married the first sibling," Satariel answered.

"My team's, and my, mates are, all, the second child," Kobabiel added.

"They were not 'spirit' mates." Batman answered Brock's question.

"How do you know?" Brock asked.

Batman tilted his head and squinted. "They died."

Everyone else nodded their heads in

agreement. If they had been 'spirit' mates, Michael never would have let that happen. He would have saved them just like he saved Robyn, Symphony and Hope. They could count on Michael's word.

Brock nodded his head, too. "So, did you know they'd been killed, Satariel?"

"I knew they were in Paradise. As you are aware, Sammael, the death angel, allows me to escort all of my descendents to Paradise. But when I took their mother, they were already there. They could not remember how or when they died. They did not remember that children had been, violently, stolen from them. They did not even remember they'd had a child." Every one could hear the pain in his voice. Satariel was hurting over this tragedy.

No one questioned why Sammael hadn't contacted Satariel. They all understood that he allowed Satariel the privilege but he had to be on the scene when they died. Sammael would not seek Satariel out, as a courtesy. History recorded Sammael right! He was neither good nor evil...he was dispassionate. But why couldn't he have just called the man! But they knew the answer to that question, too. Had Satariel been there in advance, he would have killed Destiny's father before he could kill her natural mother. That would have been wrong, because life's hand has to be played.

~

Everyone was blown away by Ali's next statement. "Righteous retribution is *yours*, Satariel." Sure they were Destiny's and Nantan's mothers, but they were Satariel's grandchildren. Not only had they been horribly murdered, they'd been denied the escort of their grandfather's gentle hand. That trumped his righteous retribution on every level.

The lump in Satariel's throat was choking him. He could barely speak. He wanted this bastard so badly, he could taste it. But he wouldn't have infringed on Ali's right. "Thank you, Bezaliel." He would never forget Ali's yielding of that right to him.

"We have wasted *too* much time," Arak said. They'd planned months ago to combine forces with Satariel's team and wage an all out war on the Fallen. They'd discussed it in the creepy castle, in New Jersey. Yet, here they sat, almost a year later, still waiting on Satariel's strategist to show up.

Arak hated procrastination. "When is Ron gonna get his butt here? Look at all those innocent women being slaughter, Satariel! Either he comes now or we plan around him!"

"I say we go without him. You don't *need* his help strategizing, Arak," Chaz said. "You are the best damned strategist in all of creation. Hell, everybody knows that, man!" He didn't understand why he thought he needed Ron, in the first place. "Besides, even if Mark can't do battle, he can damn sure help you plan it."

"Yeah, I agree! If Mark can knock all the balls off a pool table in one swing, just image him planning to take down the Fallen," Ram said, proud of his brother-in-law.

"That's right! We can handle this," Dan said.

"Ron is a capable strategist, too," Satariel spoke up for his man. "Unfortunately, fatherhood has his attention. You will all learn that that is not an uncommon behavior. I was the same way and I'm sure Brock has been too."

"Not really," Brock said. "But, we all live under one roof, so Jodi has a lot of help with the girls. You should have let Ron bring Elizabeth and the children here, when Arak offered, Satariel. That way Ron could be about his business without worry for his family."

Satariel knew Brock was right. His only comeback was, "So you could steal him, too?"

Brock shook his head. "I would not have stolen him; just like I didn't steal Donnell. You said all the members of your team married first born 'spirit' mates, right?"

Satariel nodded his head.

"Desiree was the third sibling. Her two older siblings died. So, Donnell evidently was *supposed* to be on my team," Brock informed him.

Satariel looked at Donnell. "She's the third?"

Donnell nodded. "Yes."

"Well damn!" Satariel said, shaking his head.

~

As always, Doc had a calm head. "Why don't we deal with what's going on in Montana right now. These are humans. We don't need to strategize to deal with them."

"That's true," Batman said. This cause was dear to his heart. They were sacrificing innocent young women. "Let's just wipe them out and be done with it. Hell, we could be home by breakfast."

Everyone nodded their heads in agreement.

~

Brock furrowed his brows. He thought Ali had seen it. He'd thought they'd all seen it. But every one of them missed it! "Look again." He opened his mind once more. This time he honed in on the 'so called' Priest's face.

"Shamsiel?" They all said at once. How the hell did they miss that! He was in the temple, waiting at the altar, with his lesser demons, when the women were brought in. They hadn't, just, bled to death; their blood had, slowly, dripped into a gold chalice. Then it was handed to the *'Priest'*, as a sacrificial offering. Then he and his minions feasted off their victim's blood.

They were right, this wasn't a coincidence, but calculated. Shamsiel was trying to build an army, just as his father, before him, had tried. Except he couldn't spawn them himself, because demons didn't have the discipline Watchers had. Once they started taking a woman's blood they couldn't stop. They would drink from her, throughout the course of the rape, until they killed her. So he had to use, gullible, human men to impregnate the women. So long as they brought him the woman's child and her blood, he would not drink from his followers! He'd never been in danger of being dispatched by Watchers, because he'd never had to stalk his victims. He hid in the temple, like a lion trapped in a zoo, and let his followers bring him his meals.

~

"You know what this means, don't you?" Kobabiel asked.

"What?" Ali asked, because his mentor was looking at him, when he'd asked the question.

"The only reason Nantan's mother lived to birth him was because they knew he was a male child. I'd bet no male child was cut from their mother's womb."

Brock nodded, understanding the rational. "They didn't want to risk harming a male child, if taken too soon."

"Nantan was to be a sperm donor for Shamsiel. That's why my grandson was so angry. And that's why he beat him. Not because he is *gay*, but because Nantan would not fulfill the promise he'd made to Shamsiel," Kobabiel said.

Ali was offended. "Son of a Bastard! He pimped out his own son!"

"I believe all of his followers do. My question is why Destiny and Seke were not sacrificed, as one of the child bearers?" Satariel asked.

"Our grandson *did* love his children. He would not have offered either to be *killed.* If Nantan had gone along with him and produced an offspring, only the mother would have died. No harm would have come to Nantan or his baby."

"The mother wouldn't have been a relative so he would've had no, vested, interest in her well being," Ali added. "I wonder what would have been the outcome if he'd known Destiny's and Nantan's mothers were his distant relatives."

"So what has he done with the other male children and their mothers?" Batman asked.

"They are probably his surrogates, too. I would venture to say the medicine man was probably one of those male children," Brock said.

"I agree. The mothers who refused to give up

their sons, like Nantan's mother did, are probably dead. It's a vicious cycle," Kobabiel said.

"If that's true, how, in the world, did Shamsiel get his hands on my grandson? He certainly was *not* one of the male children!" Satariel said adamantly.

"His wife," Kobabiel said, dryly. "My son, Hania, warned his son not to marry that woman. Throughout ancient history the downfall, of many men, was caused by a woman. Starting with Eve."

Everyone started nodded their heads and remembering friends of old: Adam, Noah, Samson, Solomon, David, Elijah, even John. The list went on and one. They were all grateful they had *good* women, because their women could make them do anything, too. Human men always fell into the trap of thinking they were the stronger sex. Yeah right. From the beginning of time, women have always been running the show, men just don't know it.

~

"The first thing I want to do is destroy that, damn, temple!" Brock said. "Who would have thought all these centuries, there were still fools worshiping that crap?"

"I am assuming Satariel no longer wants the medicine man," Ali stated.

"You assume correctly." Satariel nodded.

"Okay, then Brock you can have the medicine man and Satariel can have Shamsiel. But that temple is mine!" Ali said. He wanted to destroy that false goddess, "Diana", once and for all. She was an affront to the Master.

"That's fair enough," Brock said, nodding his head. After all, it was Ali's mother-in-law's body that had been scarified on its altar.

~

Doc was equally entitled to retribution, because they were after Kwanita, too. But he was conciliatory, by nature and didn't raise a stink. He'd handle his fair share of the enemy, once they got to Montana. At the end of the day, all that mattered was eliminating the threat. Plus, if he could get his hands on that chalice, he'd be satisfied.

~

"I'm concerned about leaving Lilia with no Watchers in the house," Dan said, feeling the need to reach out and kiss her.

Ali was thankful his and Brock's bond was reaffirmed. He'd spent centuries yielding to Brock's wise decisions and it was needed now. "Destiny is not pregnant, but I agree. What do you recommend, Brock?" Ali asked. He'd waited for his mate a long time. He was not about to jeopardize her safety.

Everyone was nodding and looking to Brock for direction. "What if Hatred and his crew escape again?" Chaz asked, thinking about his, beautiful, Princess and his two sons. He shook his head. "Montana is too far away, Dawg."

"Plus our links to our women will be broken," Batman added thinking about his Sweetie, Robyn. Man, he *loved* that little woman.

As much as Ram wanted in on the battle, he wouldn't leave Precious unguarded. "I ain't going. Precious will be afraid, without me."

All of them, including Brock, were thinking the same thing. They couldn't leave their mates, unguarded. The Walkers were tough, but they were human. "I don't have to be there. I can handle the medicine man from here," Brock finally said. His twins were probably strong enough to keep everyone safe, but they were babies. That was too much responsibility for them. He wanted them to be children, as long as possible. This would be the first battle his team ever went on without him. It didn't feel right.

~

Michael appeared in the room. "You will all go. Kobabiel and I will keep an eye on the women. Kobabiel can finally meet his grandchildren and Spirit Warrior needed us both, anyway. I will also spend time with Floyd, so my presence will not appear suspicious."

"Chaz, surround the estate with your field guys, two deep," Brock said.

Chaz nodded. He didn't need the fight as bad as before, but he was looking forward to it. He dropped his shades over his eyes and smiled just before he teleported out of the conference room.

Batman and Dan gave each other a high five. They, like Chaz, loved the fight.

The rest of the team laughed at them, because they knew those boys were overdue for some serious hand to hand action.

CHAPTER 15

~

All of the Watchers informed their mates that Michael was sending them on a secret mission. This was the first time they'd be leaving their mates en masse, since they'd found them. The women were all fretting over being left without their protection. They told their women that Michael was in the house helping Hania cope with what had happened. That seemed to do the trick. They stopped worrying about themselves and started worrying about their Grandfather. They knew he must be carrying a lot of guilt.

~

The Walkers weren't that easily convinced. But Brock was able to convince them that this was the same as when he'd lost contact with Cinda. "I told you that sometimes we are called out on special assignments? This is one of those times."

"But where are you going, Seraphiel," H asked.

"I can't say."

"I don't like this, Seraphiel," H pushed.

"This will happen from time to time. We need you all to keep an eye on our women. Keep them occupied so they don't worry," Brock said.

~

"Once again, I leave Brighteyes in your care. I hope you don't mind," Doc said, to Matthew.

Matthew shook his head. "Not at all, I'll keep my *cousin* safe. We all will." Once he'd found out she was his cousin, and married, he'd immediately lost interest.

Chaz looked at Mark. "You told Princess you'd make it up to her for treating her badly. This is your chance."

"It will be my pleasure to spend quality time with Hope." Mark's smile reached his eyes. He was looking forward to it.

Batman looked at Sal and Geno. "I trust you both will stand in and help protect Robyn."

"You can count on it," Sal said.

Robyn stabbed her finger in Brock's chest. "My baby daddy better not come back here all shot up again, you hear me!" There wasn't a smile on her face.

Batman smiled, as Brock did everything he could to keep from laughing at her. Brock's lips were twitching. He couldn't speak because he'd start laughing and that would make her mad. He just nodded his head.

~

Ali was alone with Destiny. He hated to leave her, but this was for her. "I'm sorry you'll have to spend the night alone, Darlin', but I have no choice."

"I know, Ali. But promise me you will not be hurt."

Ali bent his arms, at the elbow, and flexed his muscle. "Not a chance. I still have to take you on a picnic, in the Serengeti."

She wrapped her arms around his neck. "And tell me about the Pyramids."

"Yup. Plus, I have to see you in something besides that flannel nightgown." He wrapped one arm around her and caressed her cheek with the other. "I love you, Darlin'. I have waited for you a long time."

"And now I'll wait for you." She stretched up and he leaned downward. Their lips met half way in between and they kissed, passionately.

All he wanted to do, this minute, was make love to his woman; but there wasn't time. He needed to destroy that temple, before nightfall. *"I have to go, Destiny,"* he said, but didn't stop kissing her.

Ali had to have invented kissing, because he was making Destiny's toes curl. The texture of his lips was as smooth as silk. The way he'd nibble on her bottom lip, gave her chills. *"I know,"* she finally responded, but did not pull away either.

~

"Ali, stop kissing that woman, and come on. Let's get this over with, man!" Brock called out to him.

"I was right the first time, you are a nosey bastard. Give me a minute, Dawg," Ali responded.

Then he heard all the men laughing at him. He, begrudgingly, pulled away but continued to caress her cheek.

She was beautiful. The softness of her caramel colored skin made it, almost, impossible for him to leave. He was about to kiss her again, when they both heard, *"ALI!"*

"Alright, already!" Ali responded. Then he gave Destiny a quick kiss and vanished.

CHAPTER 16

The women were out done. They knew the men hung out in this room and they'd never been invited. But they didn't know they had all these things in their "quote" "unquote", 'wolf den'. While they'd been relegated to seeing after the children, all day, the men were having fun!

"Ain't this a trip?" Amanda finally said, staring at the big screen TV, the pool and ping pong tables. "I'm babysitting Adrian's daughters while he's hanging out!"

"Don't even get me started." Lara frowned. "I teach Sylvia and Sheila and then help them with homework I assigned! All the while their father is hanging out with his boys!"

"I love my boys, but I'd like some fun time too," Hope agreed.

"Look, they even have surround sound wired all over this room!"

"It looks like it's been modeled after a 'gentlemen's' club!" Lucinda added. "This is not fair!"

"Damn straight, it ain't!" Jodi added, looking at the card table. "When's the last time any of us, women, played a hand of Bid?"

"Look at these bar stools," Robyn said stroking them. "They are softer than the ones in the kitchen."

"There's going to be some changes around here!" SnowAnna said, staring at all the men.

~

The men were all afraid to speak up for themselves. All of them looked at Hezekiah; as if to say, "*defend us*"! But Hezekiah's mother didn't raise him to be a fool. He kept his trap closed and let the women rant. But Seraphiel and the team might have a surprise when they get back. If he knew his wife, when she said changes, she meant changes!

Sal finally spoke up. "If you ladies like, we can make a room for you all."

"Yeah, like what kind of room?" Sasha asked.

"Whatever you want, Honey," Elijah said eagerly.

"There are plenty of rooms still available that we can turn into a room for you ladies," Howard added.

"There are none as big as this one!" Earlie said. Then she looked at Luther. "Are there!"

"No, but, Honey, this is Brock's house. He picked this room for us guys."

"This ain't Brock's house!" Jodi frowned. "This is all our homes. He doesn't get to choose which room he wants before giving us a chance to decide!"

The men were all thinking 'damn' they were in trouble here. Geno was laughing his butt off. "Brock just might have a fit when he, gets back and, finds his den has been taken over, by a bunch of hens."

"HENS!" All the women shouted at the same time.

The older Walker men were looking at him, with their mouths open. It was obvious Geno didn't know a, *damn,* thing about women.

"Oops! Did I say that out loud?" He, abruptly, stopped laughing.

The younger Walker's fell out laughing at

him. Ditto was frowning, "Did your tonsils like meeting your foot, Eugene?"

"You play too much, boy!" Nantan hit him upside the head. "Now you've got us all in trouble."

"And since you think it is funny, here's what's going to happen, Adrian." Amanda frowned. "I will keep the girls as long as you are working on the construction site. When you come in, guess who will be seeing after his own children?"

"That goes for you too, Sam!" Lara scowled at her, still laughing, son.

"And guess who will be keeping their nieces?" Sasha said, with her hands on her hips. "Leroy?"

"And nephews?" Lucinda added. "Henry and *'Ditto'*." They knew she meant business, because she never once called Howard 'Ditto'. She hated that pet name.

"This room *would* look good as a spa, wouldn't it?" Jodi said looking around.

"We could have our own steam room," Aurellia said.

"And section off a part for aroma therapy," Symphony added.

"Hair and nail section, too," Hope said. "I'll manicure everyone's nails.

"I'd like one of the deep tissue body massage tables, and chairs," Destiny added.

"I do good massages!" MeiLi said. "I give all women massage."

~

The women were going on, and on, about their plans for this one large room. The men were standing around, wanting to cry. They were, all, thinking *women ruin everything*! But none of them were as silly as Geno to say it out loud.

"This room would look good with a nice soft, soothing color, like...peach!" Sasha said.

Hezekiah, Howard and Luther looked at Elijah, and almost burst out laughing. He'd complained to them, all his married life about *peach shit*! He was so sick of that damned color; you couldn't pay him to even *eat* a peach. All of them had nice masculine rooms like navy blue and ivory, hunter green and tan or black and burgundy. He was stuck with, sissified, peach...and peach!

When they'd finally been reunited, after the ten years, they'd asked him what color his bedroom had been for all that time. He'd scowled and said, *"She forgot me! She forgot her children! Hell, she forgot her, own, damn name! But I'll be damned if she didn't remember she loved the color peach!"* They'd, all, laughed so hard, they cried.

Now they all turned their back to keep from laughing at the expression on their poor, emasculated, brother's face.

~

Elijah knew his brothers were laughing at him. He was thinking if he sees one…more…peach room he was going to flip a, frigging, blood vessel! He loved Sasha, but enough with the damn peach, already! It was bad enough he had to sleep in a bedroom, with a peach comforter, peach walls, peach chairs and peach drapes. What the hell was it with her and all this damn peach! Of course, he'd never say that out loud. He hadn't complained, out loud, anyway, in forty years, no reason to start now. Although in the past he'd known he could, one day, escape peach…when he died. But, according to Brock, none of them would die. He sighed, and said out loud, "Oh Lord, help me."

His brothers rushed out of the room, laughing. They had to leave before the women wanted to know what was funny. They could be heard, going down the hall, howling.

~

Floyd, Michael, Hania and Kobabiel were in Floyd's office…laughing at the men. They could hear everything going on, because Michael needed to keep an eye on things. It was too funny not to share with his three friends.

"Poor Elijah." Floyd laughed.

"You all know SnowAnna is stubborn. Bet money, in a minute, we will start hearing furniture being moved." Hania laughed.

Sure enough! They heard what sounded like chairs or a table scraping the floor. The four of them laughed that much harder.

~

Hezekiah, Howard and Luther walked in Floyd's office planning to tell them what was going on. Howard and Luther had already met Michael, earlier. But one look at their faces, they realized they already knew. Everyone burst out laughing again. At Elijah.

"Why doesn't Elijah just tell Sasha he is sick of all that peach?" Hania asked and then laughed.

"Don't know." Hezekiah sat down in one of the chairs. "But here's the bigger issue. It would be unfair for our boys to come back and find out the women have taken over their room."

Michael burst out laughing. "Don't use them as an excuse. You know you just want to keep that room!"

"Well that's true, too. But come on man; break us off a little compassion."

"What did you have in mind, H?" Floyd asked.

Hezekiah, Howard and Luther all said at the same time, "Distraction!" And all looked at Kobabiel.

"You mean me?" Kobabiel laughed.

"Yup!" All four Walker brothers said, without shame.

"It really would be a shame for the team to come back and have no place to relax," Floyd said with a smile on his face. He liked the room just as much as the rest of the men.

~

The women had the younger Walker boys move the pool table over against the outer wall. They wanted to measure how much floor space they had to work with. None of their sons had the nerve to refuse. Even Sal was putting his muscles in it.

The men were all thinking you might as well put a casket in the middle of the floor, because they were all grieving. This room had been perfect. It was in the wing where the singles guys all lived. It was away from the children…and the, hormonal, women. This was their room and it wasn't fair! They were being bullied by a bunch of women! Howbeit some of those women were their mothers, but still!

~

"What have we here?" Michael said, walking in the room.

"Hi, Michael," everyone said at once.

"I believe there are several people I haven't had the pleasure of meeting," Michael said, walking towards Sal.

Sal was trembling. My God, he never would have imagined, in all his life, he'd be privileged to meet this Angel. He went to bow down, but Michael stopped him.

"There is no need for that." Then Michael shook his hand. "I am just the messenger. The Master has always known your heart. Spend time with Floyd so he can get you up to speed. The Master has need of your services."

Sal's eyes watered. That's all he'd ever wanted to do was be in the service. He nodded his head.

Then Michael walked over to, a nervous, Nantan and extended his hand. "Mark told you correctly. God has found favor in you. In spite of what your parents put you through, your name has been written in the Lamb's Book of Life. Be at ease."

Nantan was speechless. His parents were WRONG! He was not NOTHING! He wasn't going to hell! His eyes welled.

Michael smiled at Destiny and bowed. "Your devotion to your brother caused the balcony of heaven to lean downward. All of the Angels wanted to see the face of the woman who, like a good Sheppard, left all she had…for the one."

Then Michael grabbed her hand and entwined it in Nantan's. "Continue to hold each other's hand. There will be some dark moments ahead. But you will get through them, together. Ali, Geno and this household, will see that you do."

That was cryptic as all get out, but Michael moved on to Geno and started laughing. "You bring laughter with your antics! The Master likes that. You stood by and protected Sal, even though he denied being your father. You honored your father and that pleased the Master. There is a time to kill, but you would not let your friends kill Robyn, because she was innocent. The Master approves of you."

For once Geno kept his mouth shut! But his eyes watered, nonetheless.

Michael turned around and addressed everyone else in the room. "Robyn, Lucinda, Earlie, Lorraine and Renee, it's a pleasure meeting all of you. Renee, Richard will be just fine."

Then he opened his arms. "Granddaughter."

Aurellia walked in. "Hi, Grandpa Michael."

"Keeper of my heart."

"Hey, Michael."

He went down the line. "Howard, Matthew, Leroy, Luther, Sam, Paul, Tim, Addison, Adrian, Aden, Mark, Deuce. Good to see you young men again."

"Hey, you didn't speak to me and my brotha!" Jason pouted his lips.

"I am sorry. Jason, Jonathan, Sylvia, Sheila, Autumn, Summer, Adriana, Justine, it's good to see you all, too."

"How are you doing, Sasha?"

"I'm fine, Michael." She felt honored to be called by name.

Michael smiled. "Good. That's good. Your husband is going crazy with all that peach in his bedroom. The Master thought you would want to know."

Elijah's jaw dropped. His brothers burst out laughing.

Michael turned and looked at SnowAnna. "There are some people here, who you are long overdue meeting."

"Who?" Jodi asked, thinking maybe Brock

should be here.

~

Hania walked through the door with his father, Kobabiel, and his mother, Kiche. Hania smiled and said, "These are all my children."

"Children, these are my parents, Kobabiel and Kiche."

~

Everyone stood still and stared at the striking couple. They both looked around Nantan's and Destiny's age. Kobabiel was tall dark, Italian and built like Hania. Kiche was almost as tall, stout and Indian.

SnowAnna walked over and hugged Kobabiel. "I saw you. You saved E-du-di from Hatred."

Kobabiel hugged her. "No. Not me. You saved Hania."

SnowAnna frowned. "I couldn't have."

"You were there. I saw you. You were telling your father not to let Hatred touch him. Hania and I both saw you, SnowAnna. More importantly, Hatred saw you and ran. He knew only love could make you project your spirit to save your father. It was you."

Everyone gasped.

SnowAnna refused to accept it. "I can't do that!"

"You were there, little girl. Hatred ran from you, not my father," Hania told her. "When you fainted, in my arms, it was caused by your spirit rejoining your body, child."

Hezekiah was staring at SnowAnna. It had to be true. Hania had secretly shared with him that SnowAnna didn't really need a vision quest. All she had to do was meditate and she could see past, present and future. But Hania hadn't told him she could do this! "Just before you fainted, you drew a deep breath, Snow. My God, how did you do that?"

"I don't know. I didn't know I did," SnowAnna whispered.

"You have come into your own, SnowAnna. Don't be frightened of this gift. Embrace it, but do not abuse it," Kobabiel said.

~

The women were no longer interested in the 'wolf den'. They surrounded Kobabiel and Kiche and bombarded them with a million questions.

Kobabiel had previously told Kiche what the women were doing in that room. He also told her that the men were using them as bait to stop it! She'd laughed but agreed to help. "I'd like to see the rest of the house. I understand it's quite impressive," she said innocently. "And I'd like to meet Elizabeth and Hannah, if I may, Jodi."

That did it! They all left to give her a tour and let her meet the babies. The chatter going down the hall was music to the men's ears, because it was moving farther and farther away.

Michael looked at the men and laughed. Then he said, "You all can put the pool table back where it belongs. They will not return before the team gets back."

The younger men jumped right on it. They wanted to hug Michael. "Good looking out," Ditto said.

"Michael, I can't believe you told my wife!" Elijah said.

"*You* should have. Sasha is not an unreasonable woman." Michael laughed. "Besides, I move at the Master's command. Didn't you say, 'Oh Lord, help me'?"

"Yeah but that was just an expression."

"To the Master it was a supplication."

Elijah's brothers started laughing, again. "Man, you should have seen your face. I swear I heard your jaw drop!" Luther said.

Even his son and nephews started laughing at him. He'd stood there and refused to make eye contact with Sasha. She'd kept trying to quietly get his attention...he kept looking at the floor.

Nantan rested his elbow on Elijah's shoulder. "I'll be wondering what's going on in your bedroom tonight, Uncle."

Elijah looked at the smile on Nantan's face, and started laughing. "Me too, since I probably won't be sleeping in there."

"Then it's a good thing we still have our 'wolf den' ain't it." Mark laughed. "Look on the bright side. She'll be so mad at you, that she won't remember they wanted to take our room." Mark kept laughing.

"But what if it's just a momentary reprieve?" Addison asked.

"Let's just hope Brock is man enough to

stand up to Jodi!" Matthew said.

"Oh please, that woman has that man whipped!" Hezekiah laughed.

"Just like the rest of our women do!" Howard admitted. "I already told y'all I ain't shame."

~

Everyone laughed at him, but Ditto.

CHAPTER 17

Ditto liked the way his father openly confessed his love and devotion to his mother. He'd always told them their mother owned him and that he'd do anything to hold on to her. Ditto understood that, because Naomi certainly owned him. "Hey dad, I'm getting married!"

Howard smiled from ear to ear. "I knew it! The way you cut out of here, I knew it!"

"You didn't waste any time, did you, Nephew?" Elijah teased.

Ditto decided to tell them what happened. "I went over there prepared to get on my knees and beg her to marry me. I'd been carrying her ring in my pocket, since the day she left. But when she'd opened the door, the first thing she'd said was, "Marry me, Howard." She was crying and apologizing for leaving me."

"Aw snap! She asked you?" Addison asked. "That's the kind of woman I want!"

"That's the kind of woman we all want,"

Leroy said.

"You'll do well with anybody, as long as it ain't that Ms. Lilith!" Aden said frowning.

"What is it with you and Lilith, Aden?" Adrian asked. "From day one you didn't like that girl." He'd never seen his brother have such distaste for anyone, like he did her.

"She's evil!" Aden said, boldly.

"You don't know that!" Leroy tried to defend his ex-girlfriend.

"Trust me I know," Aden said, with conviction. "I know."

"How?" Matthew asked. He'd met the woman, just like they all had. They didn't see anything wrong with her.

Michael was still in the room, listening to their conversation. "You, all, will do well to heed Aden's words," he said.

Everyone turned around and looked from Aden to Michael. "What?" Leroy asked. "What's wrong with her?" He looked from Michael to Aden and back.

"This woman that you speak of would not be able to enter these gates."

That meant one thing, demonic. Leroy stumbled backward. If it weren't for his father, he would have landed on the floor. "Who the hell have I been dealing with, for the past three years?" he asked staring at Aden.

Aden stared right back. "Lilith!"

"Who is she? What is she?" Leroy was, almost, pleading.

"I don't know the who. But I do know the what. She is pure evil!"

"How could you know that, son?" Justin asked.

"She vexed my spirit like no one has ever done. Whenever I was in her presence, I had the desire to, strenuously, pray," Aden replied. Then he frowned. "Not for me…for you, Leroy!"

"Why didn't you say something?" Leroy asked.

"Would you have listened?" Aden asked. "I did what I was compelled to do…pray!" Then he explained, "All the time you were with her, she was scheming and plotting. Exactly what, I don't know. But I know one thing…she's evil to her very core, cuz."

"How do you know she was scheming?" Mark asked.

"She kept asking questions about things that didn't concern her."

"Like what?" Adrian asked. "People inquire all the time. What was so strange about her inquiries?"

"She asked, too many, questions about our family. People she hadn't met and probably never would."

"Like who?" Nantan asked.

Aden paused and, then, looked under-eyed at Nantan. "You."

"Me!" Nantan frowned.

"She never asked me about Nantan," Leroy said.

"Because Nantan isn't really related to you, but he is my cousin. Look at him and look at me, even I can see the resemblance. I mean he's older, but we both look like E-du-di."

"That's true," Nantan said, nodding his head. "But what did she want to know about me?"

"If my family knew where you were. Had we heard from you? She said she was from Montana."

"Montana? She told me she was from Maine! What the hell did she want with Nantan?"

"I don't know. But every time she saw me she was always asking about him. Once she even accused me of lying. She told me if she ever found out I wasn't telling the truth she'd do something bad to me."

"What!" everyone said, at the same time.

Aden nodded. "Yeah, but I told her don't get it twisted. I ain't got no problem given a woman a beat down!"

"Aden!" Justin couldn't believe his son said that. "You did not tell that woman that!"

"Yes I did. And I meant it too! She was trying to intimidate me, Dad. I just wanted her to know she had the wrong guy. That was a couple of years ago. I was only twenty-one. I hadn't been called into the ministry yet." He smiled sheepishly.

"Why didn't you ever tell me about this, Aden?" Adrian asked. Aden was his brother. Nobody, male or female, messed with his little brothers.

"Please. I could handle her. But the thing is, I never found out why she was so interested in

Nantan. I was only nine when we lost contact. I didn't know how much we looked alike until he showed up. Now it makes sense that she'd kept hounding me. No matter where I went she'd be there." Then he paused. "It was almost like she was stalking me."

Justin didn't like the sound of that. "Where is she now, Leroy?"

"I don't know. I haven't seen her in months. After I made it known I wasn't interested in getting married, she said she was moving back home. But who the hell knows where home is?"

Ditto didn't like the fact that this woman was after his friend. Especially, since she was evidently from Montana. "Exactly where in Montana did she say she was from?"

"She didn't. But I do remember her saying Nantan had a debt to pay there."

"What kind of debt?" Nantan asked.

"That's what I asked her," Aden said. "Then her eyes..." He paused and raised his hand. "...I swear to God, went black...like a demon's. After that, I started praying every time I saw her."

"Well at least she's left town," Hezekiah said.

"No she hasn't. I saw her the day before we moved in here. She's still scurrying around."

Ditto turned towards Michael. "What is she?"

"She's a demon possessed human."

"What does she want with Nantan?"

"That is nothing for you to worry about. If I am not mistaken, she is back in Montana."

Hezekiah had been around Michael enough to read between the lines. "Exactly where have you sent Brock and the team, Michael?"

"Montana."

CHAPTER 18

The team stood, invisible, in front of the Temple. It was almost an exact replica of the Grecian styled temple built 550 BC. The only difference was this temple actually had enclosed walls, whereas the original one did not. There were six marble steps that were the length and depth of the temple. There were also rows, upon rows, of stone columns standing side by side going the length and depth, as well. The columns gave the appearance of a wraparound porch, similar to the one at the estate.

Even without going inside the walls, the team knew there pillars lined up symmetrically to the ones outside. Whoever built this thing had put a lot of money and time into it. Too bad it was coming down today!

Hundreds of worshippers were gathered on the steps, on every side, waiting for the sun to go down. It was amazing to the team that these people could worship a God who couldn't tolerate the sun.

Rationale should dictate that if you were God, you created the sun. Wouldn't you think! But they were like sheep, mindless supplicants, going wherever their Sheppard led them. Today, it would be straight to hell.

All of them were barefooted, because it was a custom that no one could enter the faux sanctuary with anything on the soles of their feet. What a crock! But these people believed because they knew the Master had required the same thing of their friend, Moses.

When the team noticed that they were all barefooted they looked at each other and laughed. At first they didn't understand why Ali would prefer to level the temple, instead of taking out the medicine man or Shamsiel. They knew their boy wasn't a coward; after all, he was gunning for Brock, when he came in the conference room. Now they understood. This, right here, was going to be the shits, especially with the sun still up.

~

Ali felt he should be obedient to their goddess's command. It was the least he could do. Without a word, he discarded his shoes. He'd worn his least favorite ones, in case they got lost in the battle.

He stepped on the first step of the temple. The congregation, standing around, could not see him, or the team, but they heard the temple creak. It sounded like a building sounds when it settles. He, slowly, lifted his other foot and placed it on the second step. The temple trembled. Ali ascended to the third step - the temple moaned. The fourth step – the temple groaned. The fifth step – the temple cried. Finally he stepped on the sixth step and the temple screamed, in agony.

The people standing around swiftly moved down the stairs and backed away. They began whispering amongst themselves, trying to figure out what was going on. The building sounded like it was alive, and in pain.

Ali's powers were the bane of this temple's existence. He was imbued with the power to suck the moisture out of anything, including an ocean. Every step he took would reduce the cement to a dry powder. He would slowly and painstakingly bring this bastard to its knees.

Now at the top of the stairs, standing between

two pillars he shouted out to the team. *"Don't y'all think Samson's grandson would love the irony of this shit! No wonder he's my boy!"*

The team knew he meant James. They had never put that shit together, either. They all started laughing as he stretched his arms out and grabbed a hold of two of the pillars. *"They made a mockery of your death, Mama. I can't cope with that,"* he said, and siphoned the moisture until the pillars crumpled and fell at his feet.

~

The building was screaming to the top of her lungs. She knew she was dying. The people on the ground began to scream and cry out, "Master, the temple!" No one answered their cries.

~

Shamsiel and his minions were inside wondering what the hell was going on. They could hear the building screaming and feel it trembling. They heard their followers outside screaming and begging them to help. But as long as the sun was up, they were trapped.

~

Ali took his time and walked in between two

of the inner pillars. With every step he took, the foundation was crumpling under his feet.

There were close to one hundred twenty pillars and he knew he'd never destroy them all, before the sun went down. But he was, methodically, attacking the ones that were the main support beams. His feet were doing enough damage that once the supports were gone, this house of horror would come crumpling down. Just as his friend, Samson, had done, he planned to bring it down on the demons' heads. Except unlike, Samson, he would not die! More than anything, he wished James could be here, helping him, for the memory of the child Lara had been when these bastards had traumatized her!

One day Ali was going to remember that Michael hears everything!

~

"James, may I have a private word with you," Michael said.

"Sure." James walked away from the Walker men who were still discussing Lilith.

Michael did not speak out loud; nor did he mince his words. He spoke to James' mind. He told him everything. Including where the team was and what they were up to.

James turned pale and his eyes watered; not for Nantan and Destiny, but for his Lola. She'd been just a *little* girl! He nodded his head, and vanished.

Hezekiah had been watching them, all the while, and saw the expression of James' face. Then he'd vanished. "Where did James go, Michael?"

Michael answered with one word. "Montana."

~

James appeared on the landing of the temple, right next to Ali; even though he couldn't see him. "Where are you, Dawg?" he called out to his friend.

Ali cursed, "Son of a Bastard! What are you doing here, James?"

"Michael heard your request. Thanks for the invite!"

Brock and the team all uncloaked themselves, because James was exposed, out in the open.

~

The crowd started screaming, "Demons! Demons! Help us, Master!" The women tried to run, but Brock wrapped a binding shield around them, trapping them. No one was leaving this place, at least not alive. It should have disturbed him that he'd have to kill women, but it didn't. Now he understood Sal when he'd said he'd never killed anyone innocent, be they male or female.

~

James could not suck the moisture out of the pillars, like Ali, but they all watched as his actions were reminiscent of his grandfather, Samson. It was a beautiful sight to see, as he wrapped his arms around two pillars, and pulled. With the speed of light the pillars fell, like a bird without wings.

"Damn!" Ali said. "Here I am working my ass off draining the life line out of these pillars and you just snapped them in half."

James laughed. "If motivated, I can have all these pillars down, in less than ten minutes!"

"Do you, Dawg." Ali laughed. "I'll go for the outer walls." He gave James a knuckle bump and walked toward the wall.

~

"Who is that?" One of the minions asked. The demons could hear the noise going on outside. They knew what was happening. They just didn't know who was behind it. They all wished they had somebody…anybody they could pray to, to make the sun go down now!

When the outer wall started crumpling they ran to the far side of the building and hoped they were not in direct line with the sun. If they were, there would be no need to teleport out, because they'd be blind. They wouldn't be able to see where they were teleporting to. Then it hit them. "It can't be Watchers! They can't tolerate the sun any more than we can!" Another minion said.

"So who the hell is it?" Shamsiel asked. "If it's humans I'm going to drain the life blood out of them!"

~

James was busy destroying the pillars when he heard a woman shout his name. "James! Help me! Don't you know me? I'm Lilith! I'm Leroy's girlfriend."

All the Watchers turned around and stared. They hadn't heard the story Aden told, but they knew he said she was evil. "Well, I'll be damned!" Brock said. "Lilith, long time no see, girl!"

Lilith recoiled. "Seraphiel! I should have known you were behind this."

"What are you doing hanging around these demons!" Brock asked, walking up to her. Lilith wasn't a demon, because, like Watchers, demons were male. He never really knew where she came from. Some claimed she was Adam's first wife, but that wasn't true. Others claimed she was once an Angel that decided she didn't like living in heaven. He doubted that, too. Who would want to leave heaven? One thing he did know was that she was an ambassador for the fallen and was as old as time.

James walked up next to Brock. "Lilith, I just had an interesting conversation with Aden."

Lilith moved further back in the crowd. "He's a liar!"

"I haven't told you what he said. Why are you calling him a liar?"

"Because he never liked me!"

"What did he say, James?" Brock asked.

"You tell me," James said, giving Brock

permission to read his mind.

Brock did just that and then frowned. "You threatened my nephew?"

Lilith swallowed hard. "I didn't know he was related to you, Seraphiel!"

"And I supposed you didn't know Nantan was my peeps, either?"

Lilith was vigorously shaking her head. "No!"

The crowd could see the fear on her face. Brock was glad for once that his reputation had superseded him. Lilith knew what he was capable of and knew what he was going to do to her.

~

He was just about to dispatch her when Raphael appeared. "No, Seraphiel. Hell will not hold this creature."

"What can I do with her then? We cannot let her continue to roam the earth. Look at the destruction she continues to cause."

"I will take her and bind her, like I did her mate," Raphael said and grabbed Lilith by the arm.

"Who is her mate?" Brock asked.

"Azazel," Raphael said. "She was once

human, but Azazel turned her into this," he said and revealed her true form. The humans started screaming and moving away from her.

"Maaaa! Maaaa! Neah!" Lilith cried, sounding like the creature, she'd sold her soul to become…a goat woman! She was shaking her head from side to side. "Maaaa!"

Brock jumped back. Azazel was, way, more powerful than him. He wondered if this creature was, too. He knew, for certain, that Aden wouldn't have been a match for her. "Say what?"

Raphael laughed. "Just imagine how Leroy will feel, if he ever finds out what she really looks like."

The team started laughing. But, Brock was shaking his head. "Nawl, we can't do that to him." He could envision Leroy throwing up for the rest of his life. He would!

"Anyway, you guys better get back to work. The sun will be down in a second. That is unless you want me to push it backward for you?"

Damn, Brock hated to be given options! If Raphael kept the Sun up, James and Ali could finish tearing the temple down and force the demons to go blind. But what fun would that be to fight a demon, that couldn't see you whipping his ass! "You did that on purpose, Raphael!"

Raphael was laughing. He knew Seraphiel would struggle with that. "How about this? I will take this creature and all the humans off your hands and let you deal with the demons."

Brock looked over the crowd and saw the medicine man. Damn, Raphael just did it again. But what the hell. "Alright, take them all. But you see the medicine man, over there?" He pointed at the man trying to hide behind his followers.

"I know! I know what he has done. It will be my pleasure to handle him profusely. He will get the same treatment and end up in the same place Michael placed Carl."

That satisfied both Brock and Satariel. "Thanks, Raphael."

Raphael vanished with Lilith and the humans in tow.

~

"There's not much day light left, James. The demons will be coming out in mass. Are you sure you are up to it, or do you want me to send you home?" Brock asked, concerned for his brother-in-law.

"Nah, man. Lola was only nine years old!" His eyes started watering, again. "She was only *nine*!"

"I know." Brock understood how he felt.

"I gotta do this, Dawg," James said, and walked back and started viciously pulling down the pillars.

The team was watching him in amazement. Unlike his grandfather, he knew how to pull, without bringing the whole damn thing down on his head. But then again, his sons were in construction and demolition. They probably got in that field for this very reason.

~

"I don't know about you guys, but I've got some business on the other side of that wall," Satariel reminded them. He knew they were waiting, because they didn't want the whole damn thing to come down on their heads; but he couldn't wait any longer."

"Give me a couple more minutes," Ali shouted out to him. "I'm just about done!"

"Make it quick!" Satariel said.

~

The demon could now hear them talking and knew their ass was grass! They'd spent their entire existence behind walls like this. They'd always taken the easy way out and had never learned how to fight. One of the minions whispered, "Is that Satariel, out there?"

Shamsiel was trembling. "Yeah! How did he find out about this place?"

"I don't know, but he's gonna get your *ass*. You know that, right?"

Shamsiel was, nervously, nodding his head.

"It's dark now. Let's get the hell out of here!" One of his minions shouted. They tried to teleport out, but they were all locked down!

"Son of a bitch!" Shamsiel whispered. He didn't want Satariel to hear his voice. Maybe he didn't know he was in here. Shit, who was he fooling?

CHAPTER 19

"Let's do it!" Brock said, seeing that Ali, and James, had all the pillars down.

Satariel was the first one in the building. He looked around until he saw his target squatting in the corner. "Shamsiel!" he shouted, and grabbed him, by the collar. "You low life piece of dog shit!"

"Satariel. How you been, brother?"

"Don't you dare brother me!" Satariel smacked him in the face.

"Ouch!" Shamsiel cried.

~

"Ouch?" Chaz frowned. "What the hell kind of demon hollers ouch!"

"Punk ass ones!" Satariel said. "Shamsiel was a cowardly punk when we were growing up, and he's still one!"

"That is the truth, Brother. That's why I didn't want to be a Watcher. I never learned how to fight!"

"But you found great pleasure in killing my

granddaughters! Your grandnieces!"

"No. No. No. I didn't kill them."

Satariel slapped him again. "I saw you, you sorry bastard. I saw all the women you had slaughtered!"

"Okay! Okay! Yeah I did that! But by the time they were brought here, they were already dying or dead! I needed them!"

"For what? You don't need blood to survive. Why were you drinking their blood?" Brock asked.

"To make it look authentic!" Shamsiel confessed. "To make it look like they were being offered up to the gods!"

In truth he was no more than a cowardly mouse, hiding in the dark! When Michael approached him centuries ago his response had been, *'Oh hell nawl. I ain't fighting. I don't like to get hit. Never have.'* Michael had even offered that he be a domestic, like Chef. Again he'd replied, *'No can do, Mike-Mike. I don't want to cook and clean for no damn body!'*

But he'd been able to convince human zealots that he was a god. He, just like all cults leaders, was nothing more than someone who was dissatisfied with their own insignificance. In order to boost himself up, he'd been willing to destroy innocent families to achieve his goal.

The only reason he was the leader was because he was the most handsome. Silly humans put a lot of stock in the outward appearance. When he'd first appeared and they saw how handsome he was, they were his for the picking. Neither he nor his minions ever left the temple for fear of running into other demons or Watchers. None of them had ever learned how to fight. But they had to eat. The humans brought food and laid it on the altar. His favorite was pot roast, with lots of potatoes and onions! He pretended the aroma was pleasing to his nostrils; when, in actuality, it was his stomach that ached for it.

Ali couldn't believe what he was hearing. "It was one big colossal joke to you! You killed my wife's and her brother's mothers for a joke!"

"Not a joke. There's nothing funny about being born a creature you don't want to be. I couldn't beg these humans to help us. There would've been no respect! They *had* to believe we were more powerful than they were."

"So how powerful did it make you to cut babies out of their mothers' wombs?"

"I never did that!"

"You stood your ass right here and watched!" Ali shouted.

"It would have made me weak to tell them not to do it. They knew about 'Diana's' doctrine. If I would have objected, they would have known me for the phony I am. Don't you see I didn't have a choice?"

Doc was offended. "I spent just as much time as you not knowing how to fight! I never used and abused innocent humans!"

Shamsiel looked at him. "I know how your brothers used to beat you up. You evidently have bigger balls than I, Yomiel."

~

James was shaking his head. Lola had been traumatized because of a demon that was afraid of his own shadow. He snatched one of the minions off the floor. "My wife was a nine year old child, when she saw what you made her uncle do. And for what?"

Before the minion could respond, a miniature

sword appeared in his hand. It appeared to be anointed with the same power that the Watchers' battle axes were. He rammed it into the minion's heart. The creature screamed and popped his ass in hell!

~

Shamsiel started begging, "Don't let him do that to me, brother."

"Oh, he won't," Satariel assured him. "But I will." He dropped his brother to the floor, reached for his axe and pierced his heart.

~

All the other minions started scurrying around trying to get away. There were hundreds of them trying to find a way out of their hideout. They still could not teleport; and even if they could, where would they go? They hadn't been outside the temple walls in centuries. Brock wished the, gullible, humans were still around to see how cowardly their, so called, gods were.

Raphael spoke. *"They are watching!"*

~

The team was motivated now. They would put on a spectacular show for the doomed humans.

Unfortunately, for them, they would learn too late that there is only ONE God. It would be a, sorry, one sided battle, but they would kill them, nonetheless. As a matter of fact, they wanted to kill these weasels more than any other demon. They gave demons a bad name. At least the other demons were motivated.

~

Just when they thought they had killed them all, the temple started screaming again. Its floors began to cave in and the team realized there was another group of them hiding in a basement level. That was interesting! They never would have thought there'd be a basement, because the original temple didn't have one. But with the floor giving in, the pillars were coming down, which meant the roof was sure to follow. None of the Watchers, and certainly not James, would survive that concrete coming down on their heads. Doc grabbed the chalice, Ali grabbed James, and they all teleported out to the yard, just as the temple imploded.

Doc handed the chalice to Satariel. "If you destroy this, your granddaughters will get their memories back."

"That means they will remember how horrific their deaths were," Satariel replied. He wasn't sure he wanted to do that to them.

"Yes, but they will also be able to watch over their children, and future grandchildren, from Paradise," Doc said.

"What was done to them is done. It can't hurt them anymore. But I think they will be proud of the man and woman Nantan and Destiny are," Ali said, in agreement with Doc. "Destroy the chalice, Satariel, and give them that much."

Satariel held the chalice in both hands, and the team watched as his hands turned to fire. Under the heat of the flames, the chalice turned into liquid gold, and finally dissipated. A few seconds later they all heard his granddaughters' voices. *"Thank you, Grandfather."*

~

"What about those bastards in the basement?" James asked.

"What about them?" Brock answered his question, with a question.

"Are we going to just leave them there?" James asked.

Brock shook his head. "Nope! They are already in hell." Then he raised his eyebrows. "But the big question is, how did you materialize that dagger?"

James smiled. "Oh that."

Ali started laughing. "Busted."

The team looked at Ali. "You knew he could do that?" Ram asked.

"Yup!" Ali nodded. "Our boy works for Gabriel."

"What!" They all said at once.

James kept smiling. "I always thought it was strange that none of you ever asked me *exactly* how I was able to kill these bastards."

They all frowned, because that was the truth. It never crossed their minds that demons couldn't be killed by humans. Brock remembered that James and Satariel had been friends for ten years. "You knew too, didn't you?"

Satariel nodded. "I knew."

Brock shook his head. "Too many damned secrets." He didn't have room to talk, though. This mission was the biggest secret of all.

Then he teleported back to the estate. The

team followed.

CHAPTER 20

Out of habit, the team landed in the 'wolf den'. The men were doing what they normally do: playing cards, shooting pool, singing and talking. Only this time, all the women, and children were in there, also.

Leroy had his two nieces, by his side, while Lorraine was sitting at the card table. Adrian was holding Justine in his arms, and Adriana was standing by him, while he was watching Geno and Sal shoot pool. Sam was sitting in the corner, with both his girls, helping them with their homework.

Chaz's boys had been with Henry and Ditto, but when they saw him they ran and jumped in his arms. Then they, both, whispered in his ears, "Y'all in trouble, Daddy."

"Why?" Chaz whispered back.

Brock frowned. "What's going on?"

Jodi handed him both babies, then she sat back down at the card table. She didn't even kiss him, say hello or glad you're back...Dawg.

Nothing!

The team was looking at the Walkers wondering what in the hell was going on. It was obvious their women were mad at them. Not one of their women had greeted them. And what the hell were they doing in the 'wolf den', with the children!

"What's going on, Dimples?" Brock asked her, directly.

~

All the women started talking, or rather fussing, at once. Some were pointing their fingers, others had their hands on their hips, but all of them had their mouths balled, in anger.

"We are taking this room!"

"Y'all gonna start helping with the children!"

"I ain't babysitting...no more!"

"Y'all got some nerves!"

"We're turning *this* room into a spa, for us women!"

"Y'all gonna start helping with the kids, from now on!"

"This ain't just y'all house!"

~

Yap! Yap! Yap! They kept going on, and on, grumbling, complaining and voicing their demands. They were getting on Brock's, and his team's, ever loving, nerves.

~

Arak looked at Brock, and shook his head. *"I'm out!"* He felt fortunate that he lived at Jodi's house, and didn't have to deal with this. These women's mouths would get him in, so much, trouble. For once he was glad he hadn't found his 'spirit' mate, yet. Or else, he'd be stuck here, like his brothers. He teleported home, with Baraqiel dead on his trail.

The men, Walkers and Watchers, alike, envied them.

~

Brock could kill the Walkers, and their sons, for bringing these women, and children, in here. He turned around and stared at Hezekiah. *"What the hell happened, H? I leave you in charge and look what happened!"*

"It's been going on since you left. Man, we wanted to keep them close, so we brought them in here."

"Are you out of your, damn, mind? Big as this place is, you couldn't think of nowhere to take them. Like the friggin' kitchen! Hell you could have taken them to that, big ass, media room!"

"If I'm out of my mind it's because they've been running me crazy, since you left! Not to mention Geno called them a bunch of hens!"

Brock almost laughed at that. *"Damn! When is that boy going to learn to keep his trap shut?"*

"Then Michael informed Sasha that Elijah hates his peach bedroom. She's, doubly, pissed!

Brock chuckled out loud. That made the women even madder. They thought he was laughing at them.

"I know, damn, well you hear me talking to you, Wolf!" SnowAnna yelled, pointing her finger in his face.

"I'm sorry, Cutie. What did you say?" Brock stopped talking to H and started paying attention to the women, again.

"I said…" SnowAnna paused. "Oh hell, you got me so riled up, I forgot what I was saying!" She looked at the women. "What was I saying?"

The men wanted to laugh, but didn't dare.

"My mama *said...*" Lara started and then looked around. "Where is my husband?"

"Oh shit!" The team shouted. They were not used to having to teleport anybody back. They'd left the poor bastard in Montana.

Lara went to get up in Ali's face, but Destiny stepped in front of him, blocking Lara's path. Lara stopped, but frowned at Ali. He was James' best friend, hers too. She expected him to watch out for James. "I know, damn well, you didn't leave my husband, in Montana, Ali!"

"See what had happened was..." Ali started trying to explain.

"What had happened, my butt." She gritted her teeth. "If you don't get James, right now, I'm going to load your ass up with buck shots! You hear me!" She was not happy.

"No you *won't*, Lara," Destiny said, barely above a whisper.

"I'll go!" The team said, at once. Anything to get away from these, hormonally compromised, women!

They started yacking, again! Yack! Yack! Yack! "Nobody needs to go!" Jodi reminded them.

"Don't play with me, Brock. Bring James back, now!"

~

James appeared in the room, laughing his ass off. "That was just wrong, Dawg! I was wondering how long it would take you to realize you left me," he said to Ali. Then he saw the looks on, his and, everyone's faces. He turned around to see all the women back in the 'wolf den'. He talked to Ali on their private link. *"Y'all should've left me there! How bad are they?"*

"Vicious, man. Lara threatened to shoot me!" Ali complained. *"I think she would have, too!"*

James laughed. *"My woman loves me."*

"Not right now she don't! She just wanted you here to chew on your ass with the rest of us. She made my woman mad. Look at them."

James looked over at Lara, and then at Destiny. Ali was dead on. Lara was mad at Ali...Destiny was mad at Lara.

~

The women started bitching again. The fact that they'd left James behind added, unneeded, fuel to the flame.

~

Brock had had enough. "Q-U-I-E-T!" he shouted.

The room went silent, after everyone gasped.

"Don't you, dare, yell at us, Brock!" Jodi started. "Who the hel..."

Brock cut her off. "I love you, Dimples, and, lord knows, I can't live without you. But, if I hear *one* more word, I swear to God, I'm gonna render everybody mute!" He squinted, "Starting with you!" He stared right back at her. He sensed she was fixin' to curse him, on their link. "I mean it, Jodi! Not one, damned, word! Not, even, in my head, woman!"

He turned around and frowned at the men staring back at him, in disbelief. He opened a link to all of them. *"Y'all are a bunch of punks! Grow some balls, for God's sake."*

Then he turned around, and started talking to all the women. "You all cannot *have* this room." He raised his eyebrows. "And that's nonnegotiable!"

Jodi opened her mouth to protest. But one look at Brock and she backed down. Her eyes watered. Brock was bullying her. She pouted her, quivering, lips.

Brock almost gave in because he never could stand to see her cry. But not this time! "This room is in the wing where the single men live. We picked it for that very reason! These young men need a place to relax, without their mothers being, all up, in their business. Not to mention it's far enough away from the children that they won't hear things that will frighten them. We don't, just, play in here. This is our war room! We have meetings that we don't want to concern you all with. We have conversations that the children's, *little*, ears don't need to be exposed to! It was bad enough, that these children were frightened, when we were under attack. They don't need to be frightened by the words of the very people who are supposed to protect them!"

He could see the logic was starting to sink in with the women. "Now, here's what you all can do. Pick as many rooms you'd like." He turned around and looked at Ditto and Henry. "Put the construction on hold, for a bit! Whatever rooms the women choose, knock the damn walls out and make it one big room. Build them a spa and whatever the hell else they want!"

He looked over at Lorraine. "Add the renovations cost in the construction budget; with the same twenty percent mark up. But use your gold card to order whatever equipment needed. Order you guys a big screen TV, a surround sound system. The works. While you're at it order laptops for Destiny, Nantan, Geno and Sal."

She nodded. Brock had given her a, business, gold card with an unlimited credit limit, for the maintenance of the house. He never, once, asked to see the bills. He trusted her and Chef, explicitly. The only thing he'd asked was that they pay bills, on time, and not jack up his credit rating.

Brock turned, back around, and looked at the women. "But the rooms you choose, cannot be in this wing!"

That crazy Geno jumped up and pounded his fist in the air. "Yeah!"

"Shut...Up...Geno!" Brock turned around and glared at him.

Symphony raised her hand to get his attention.

"Yes?" Brock asked.

"We want to be able to get together with everybody sometimes, for recreation."

"That's fine. We can use the shelter room for that. It is basically a replica of this room."

Hope raised her hand for permission to speak.

"Yes, Hope?" Brock said.

"What about the children! You all, still, need to help us out with them!"

That offended Chaz. "I always help you with the boys, Princess. I never come in here until both of them, and you, are asleep." He was so thankful for his family; he didn't hang out with the men, until they were tucked in. "And I never will."

She smiled. That was the truth. Chaz always made sure her, and the boys got his, undivided, attention. Even though she'd be asleep, she knew when he left their room. She didn't know why she was mad at him. She didn't care about this room, one way or the other. Hormones. "I know, Baby. I was speaking up for my girls!" She reached out and kissed his heart.

"That's between y'all. That is not an issue with me and Jodi. I spend a lot of time with

Elizabeth and Hannah, and Aurellia. The children already have a playroom, in the basement. We have supplied the room with everything you all said they needed. If they need something else, just ask Lorraine to order it. How you all arrange who takes care of them and when, is an individual family decision. They are just not allowed in *here*, ever again. Or this wing; unless you are taking them to the media room." He looked hard at the women. "And neither are any of you."

~

Destiny raised her hand for permission to speak.

"Yes, Destiny," Brock said.

She turned around and started talking to the women. "Once we decide what rooms we want, we can get Faith over here to look at the space. She has a great eye for design. She can do the blueprints, and trick our room out."

That seemed to do the trick. The women started happily chatting and making plans.

"Let's go decide which rooms we want," Jodi said, taking the babies back from Brock, without making eye contact. She turned and walked out the door.

~

Hope kissed Chaz. "Hey, Baby."

"Hey, Princess." Chaz wrapped his arms around her. "I'll keep the boys, while you guys look at rooms."

She smiled. "Okay." And they walked out the room, together.

~

Destiny kissed Ali. "I've been waiting on you a long time, Ali." She mimicked his words.

"We've got a date tonight, Darlin'."

She smiled. "I know. Let me help find the rooms first, okay?"

"I'll meet you, in our room, later." He leaned down, she stretched up and they kissed. Then he watched her, as she walked out the room. His woman looked as good going, as she did coming. She was built like Lillian, with an abundance of curves, in all the right places. The sway of her hips was a wickedly tempting siren call to his nether region. *"Nice view, Darlin'."*

Destiny blushed, but kept walking. *"It's all yours,"* she teased.

He actually groaned…out loud.

~

Robyn went to walk past Batman, but he caught her arm. He shook his head. "I missed you, Kitten. Don't do that."

She pouted her lips and laid her forehead in his chest. "I'm sorry." She didn't even care that he'd called her Kitten, in public. "I missed you, too."

He flipped her on his back and walked out the room.

~

The other women walked out, without saying a word to their husbands.

The rest of the men all understood that Elijah wasn't the only one sleeping in the 'wolf' den, tonight. Their women were *warm.*

~

Addison walked over and peeked out the door. He held his hand up and motioned the men to stay quiet. When the women and children were outside of ear shot, he turned around. "Damn, Uncle Brock, I want to be like you when I grow up!"

Everybody started laughing. From that day on, all the young men would call Brock, Uncle!

"Man, why didn't y'all just tell the women the reason we chose this room?" Brock asked, looking at Hezekiah. "Now, Dimples is pissed at me!"

H hunched his shoulders. "They came in like vipers. They didn't give us a chance to say much."

"We got a reprieve when Kobabiel came in with his wife, Kiche. But as soon as they left, the women returned," Howard informed them.

"Grandma had already made us move the pool table over against the wall," Deuce said.

"What!" Ram said, indignantly. Then he started rubbing the table and inspecting it, for damages.

"So how long do y'all think we'll be in the doghouse?" Doc asked. He really loved Brighteyes and he didn't want to sleep, if he couldn't sleep with her.

"I don't know about y'all, but I plan to sleep with my woman, in my bed, tonight!" Howard said. "Even if I have to beg."

Everybody started laughing at him. He really

didn't have pride when it came to Cindy.

"I ain't begging, but I bet money, Jodi and I will sleep in the same room, tonight! Y'all really need to man up!"

"Oh please." Dan smacked his lips. "Jodi locked your ass out for a whole month! You didn't man up then, did you?"

Brock laughed. "True that." But this time he wouldn't let her do that. He'd been miserable.

"Y'all know what we should do?" Luther asked.

"What?" They all said at once.

"Let's go to bed now. So when they, finally, come in the room we will already be there," he said, as a joke. He and Earlie had agreed, years ago, never to go to bed angry. Besides this was a stupid fight. Brock had given the women full run of the entire estate, with the exception of this *one* room. But it was the nature of the original female…wanting what she was told she couldn't have.

"That way they can't lock us out!" Elijah said, liking the idea.

They all laughed at him. "I thought you were

sick of that 'peach' room, Papa." Leroy laughed.

"The room, boy! Not your mama!" Elijah laughed and walked out the room. He was serious, as a cold shower on a cold winter morning.

He could hear the guys laughing and taunting him, as he walked down the hall. He kept right on walking. He was crazy about that, sassy, Russian. He didn't want to sleep in the damn 'wolf' den. He wanted to be in his own bed, with his wife.

CHAPTER 21

Ali was in the room, waiting, when Destiny arrived. He'd, already, showered and changed clothes. "Hey, Darlin', he said, and opened his arms.

She loved herself some Ali. He was standing there with those bowed legs, turning her on from a distance. She walked into his outstretched arms, and sighed. "I hope I don't act like my cousins, when I get pregnant." She laughed.

"You stood up to Lara for your man." He laughed.

"Girlfriend had some nerve, didn't she?" Destiny was not laughing.

"She and James are my best friends, Destiny. We spend a lot of time together. She wouldn't have shot me." He kept laughing. "I can't believe I forgot and left my Dawg."

"I know she wouldn't have. I wouldn't have let her. They were all ranting about a room."

"I'm sure you wouldn't have." Ali kept

laughing, remembering how she'd beat her sister up. "Poor Brock, Jodi is really pissed at him, isn't she?"

"Yeah. Even though he was right, he yelled at her in front of everybody. That hurt her feelings. Don't ever do that to me, Ali."

After what he and Brock had just been through, Ali felt the need to defend him. It pissed him off for those women to say, '*this ain't just your house!*' Brock never, once, acted like it was. He'd generously opened the door to every single one of them, including the team. No other team around the globe lived under one roof. Brock bought the estate over one hundred years ago and from day one, he declared it was all of their homes. "The only reason he yelled was because they wouldn't shut up. Those women started yelling at us, first. Brock takes a lot of crap off of everybody in this estate, me included. It makes me mad that everyone takes advantage of his kindness. If he lost it in there, he earned that right."

Destiny could see that Ali was getting upset about what had happened. "I know they were out of control, Baby."

"Brock has never treated Jodi like that, before. That woman owns him. Hell, she threw him out their bedroom for a whole damned month. She wouldn't even tell him what he'd done wrong or why she was mad. He was walking around here looking like a lost puppy," Ali told her.

"Why was she mad?"

Ali grunted. "He forgot their anniversary."

"Silly woman. Did she not know she was depriving herself, as well?" Destiny asked, and rubbed up against him.

He groaned. "If I ever do something wrong, tell me so we can work it out. I won't yell at you, in public or anywhere else…and don't ever try to lock me out of our room. I like holding you while you sleep, Darlin'."

"Me too." She sighed. "Let's have our date in here, Ali. Just the two of us."

"You don't want to go out?"

"Wherever I am, so long as I'm with you, I'm on a date." She stretched up and he leaned down. "I missed you, Ali."

"I love you, Darlin'," he whispered, just before he kissed her.

She pulled back and started, painstakingly, unbuttoning his shirt, one button at a time. His hairy chest was as much an aphrodisiac, as his bowed legs. She ran her fingernail over his heart, and stroked the spot, where she'd bit him. "So, damn, sexy," she whispered. She reached for, and unfastened, his belt buckle. Then she pulled it out of its loops and dropped it on the floor. She unzipped his pants. He groaned, but he was thankful for the relief. Then she pulled his shirt tail, out of his pants, and finished unbuttoning it. She pushed his shirt off his shoulders and let it drop to the floor. She ran her hands over his biceps and pecs. They were rippled with taut muscles, as hard as granite. "So, damn, sexy," she whispered, again, and kissed him, in the center of his chest. His breath hitched. She ran her arms around his waist and caught the waistband of his pants and started pushing them down. "Sit," she whispered, and pushed him down on the bed. Then she squatted and removed his shoes and socks. Even his, neatly manicured feet, were sexy. She grabbed his pant legs, pulled them over his feet, and tossed them on the floor. She had, seductively, undressed her man.

She stretched his legs and positioned them on her lap. Then she started massaging his feet. She worked her way up to his, bowed, calves. There was nothing sexier than a bow legged man. She continued to work her way up. She stared kneading and kissing his firm thighs. This was the sexiest man, ever created. And he was hers until that glorious Day of Judgment!

~

Ali was in a euphoric daze, while he'd watched Destiny undress him. No one had *ever* done that. It was erotic, as hell. When she started massaging his legs he'd jumped. When she kissed his thigh, he cursed, "Damn!" He reached down, lifted her up and pulled her into his arms. His breathing was labored. He couldn't move, or he'd embarrass himself. He laid his forehead between her breasts. *"You've driven me to the edge, Darlin'."*

~

She ran her fingers through his hair and held his head to her breasts. She shivered as his, warm, breath seeped through her blouse and caressed her skin. *"I love you, Ali,"* she whispered.

~

Ali lifted his head and looked up into her eyes. Her eyes were weepy; but not from sadness. He reached up and wiped her tears. "I love you, Destiny."

His hands trembled as he, returned the favor and, slowly undressed her. Her soft, caramel, skin glistened with excitement.

~

Destiny watched Ali undress her. His fingers were trembling, but not from nervousness. She was reading his thoughts. He was trying to take his time, but he wanted to rip that, damn, blouse off. She was glad he didn't, because he'd paid too much money, for it. Never taking her eyes off him, she stepped back, and unbuttoned it and unlatched her bra. She heard him inhale when her breasts fell out of their prison. She reached behind her and unzipped her skirt. It slipped to the floor at her feet.

~

Ali was breathing heavily, as he reached out and pulled her back in between his thighs. He reached up and slid her blouse and bra off her shoulders. They both dropped to the floor. *"I have waited a long time for you, Darlin',"* he whispered to her mind, as he caressed, and suckled, her breasts.

~

Destiny sensuously moaned. After a lifetime of her mother, and sister, telling her how fat and undesirable she was; Ali was dispelling the notion. She'd always told them that their opinion of her didn't matter; but it was a defense mechanism. It had mattered, a lot, and it hurt every time they called her a cow or a pig. She'd almost married the wrong man, because they'd made her believe she couldn't do any better. *"Ali,"* she moaned.

~

Ali heard her thoughts. *"They were wrong, Darlin'. Even I am not good enough for you,"* Ali whispered to her mind, as he untied the drawstrings to her thong. Women's underwear had come a long way in five thousand years. Whoever thought of this design was a *genius,* he thought, as he removed them. Then he leaned down and kissed her belly button. He put his hands on her hips and lay back, pulling her down on top of him. Then he turned on his side, facing her and stroked her soft, welcoming, thigh. *"They were wrong, Darlin'."* He caressed and manipulated her cheeks. They were as smooth and soft as butter. He pulled her forward and thrust his hips, uniting their bodies. *"They were definitely wrong,"* he whispered, and began the slow rhythm of making love to his woman, while staring into her eyes. Her, warm, womb welcomed him with ecstatic fanfare. He leaned in and kissed her. *"I waited a long time for you, Darlin'."*

~

Destiny stared into Ali's eyes, but saw his soul. She was not in this alone; he was as desperate, as she was. She'd had thirty five years of loneliness, he'd had five thousand. He'd already told her that her lifeline was tethered to his. She would not die until that great judgment day shout out, by Gabriel. While staring into his eyes, and stroking his chiseled jaw, she whispered a prayer of thanksgiving. All men were not created *equal.* God had created and designed her mate, especially for her. She leaned back and pulled his head down to her breasts. *"Now, Baby."*

Ali accepted her invitation and first suckled and then bit down on her breast. Her womb shook, like an earthquake. Then he leaned back, because he knew she'd return the favor.

Destiny's canines extended and she bit down over his heart. They both watched, in horror, as the scene he never wanted her to see, exploded in both their mind's eyes. The more she drew on his blood, the more she saw. She moaned, as tears fell from her eyes.

~

"NO!" Ali shouted out loud. He tried to pull her away, but she had latched on, so tightly, he didn't know if she wouldn't...or couldn't let go. All he could do was hold her head, and whisper to her, screaming, mind. *"Oh Darlin', I'm so sorry."* He rubbed his hand up and down her trembling back, trying to comfort her. *"I'm so sorry."*

He analyzed that this is why she was able to take his blood. It was written that he would never be able to keep anything from her. And he would have kept this. There would have always been this lie of omission, between them. For the first time in his existence he envied Brock's abilities. He wanted to go to Hell and beat the hell out of her father, right this minute.

~

Destiny saw everything Ali was hiding from her. She saw a traumatized, Lara and, Seke. She saw her supposed mother grab a seven month old Nantan. She saw her own mother being carved up like a, damn, turkey. She saw her mate and the team punishing the cult. She saw everything.

She wasn't able to release Ali, until she heard hers and Nantan's mothers thanking Satariel for releasing their minds. She didn't say anything, she couldn't. She laid her head in the cuff of his arm and cried.

~

Destiny had cried herself to sleep. She hadn't said a word to Ali. He was fearful that she'd go back into her dark place. Thank God she hadn't. But he felt her sorrow, to the bone. He understood it, because he'd lost his mother, in that same manner. Only he'd been the villain, in his mother's death. He pulled her closer into his arms and kissed her forehead. "We'll get through this thing, together, Darlin'," he whispered.

~

Destiny came awake a couple of hours later. She'd always known her parents were evil, but she would have never imagined the magnitude of it. They'd gone on with their lives, as if they hadn't, cold bloodily, killed two innocent women. How do you look at your children, knowing you killed their mothers? All the years her father proclaimed how much he loved them, he couldn't have loved them and deprived them of their real mothers, too.

All those years their mother, or that woman, had taunted her about being big and fat. It was a taunt at her real mother. Did her mother know her father was insane, before she'd lain down with him? Had she been so insecure that she'd settled for stolen moments, with someone else's husband? Or did she think they had a future together?

And Nantan! They'd wanted to breed him; like a prize stallion obligated to sire the next generation. She remembered her E-du-di's words, *'you went to great lengths to bring that boy into the world.'* Oh God, E-du-di had known all along! That's why he'd kept a watchful eye on her and Nantan.

311

When they were growing up, if their mother, that woman, started in after the two of them, E-du-di would show up, out of nowhere. She'd always known that her E-du-di had a second sight. Now it was apparent, he'd kept that second sight trained on them! Every, single, time that woman tried to beat them he'd show up before she could lay a hand on them. He'd never once had to say a word, but the tension between the two of them was obvious, even to a child. That woman would take one look at E-du-di and recoil, like a snake. Why didn't he tell them? Why didn't he do something?

Ali was listening to her thoughts. *"He couldn't, Darlin'. They had his hands tied. He didn't find out about it until it was already over. He was afraid your father would go to jail and you, and Nantan, would be stuck with her."*

"Ali, how could they do it? How could they kill our mothers?" She started crying, again.

"I don't know, Baby. I don't know."

Destiny remembered what Michael had told them. *'There will be some dark moments, ahead.'* She shook her head. "We have to tell Nantan. He has a right to know, Ali."

Ali had learned his lesson. Truth won't be denied. "Alright, Darlin'. We'll tell him together."

CHAPTER 22

Brock walked in his suite, prepared to grovel. He'd talked a good game, in the 'wolf den', but it was just talk! He couldn't stand Dimples being mad at him. He'd talked that crap about *man up,* but please, he wasn't even half a man, without her.

At least Howard was honest about Cinda. Every man in the den had laughed at him, but every one of them felt the same way about their woman.

Brock went to the nursery to check on the girls, first. Even that was a lie. He went into the nursery because he hoped they'd tell him how angry their mother was.

"Hey, little, girls." He smiled down on them.

They both said, at the same time, *"Hey meanie."* Only this time they didn't giggle or smile.

He pouted his lips. *"Y'all mad at me, too!"*

"You made our mommy cry!" Hannah said. She was, usually, the playful one, but not now.

Brock's heart lurched. Jodi didn't cry, when

she was mad. She'd yell and scream at him, but not cry! She only cried when she was happy...or hurt. Damn, he'd hurt her, again.

"You need to leave us and go fix it, Daddy," Elizabeth said.

He picked them up, one at a time, and kissed their cheeks. *"Tomorrow the three of us are going to hang out, okay?"* he promised them.

"Okay." They both smiled.

~

Brock walked into the bedroom and closed the door. Jodi was in bed; lying on her side, with her back to the door. And although she didn't stir, he knew she wasn't asleep. He stood with his back up against the door, and watched her. He didn't try to hear her thoughts, or read her mind. He didn't, even, try to speak to her mind; he just stood there, and watched her.

Everything he did, he did for her; including setting up the 'wolf' den. He knew how overwhelmed she felt, at times, with everybody under one roof. And even though the estate was twenty thousand square feet, per floor, sixty relatives was a lot to have living under one roof!

Not to mention Hezekiah and Deuce, or SnowAnna and Sarah were always intruding, on their privacy, trying to get to the girls. She never complained, but he knew his woman. Although he and the team basked in all the company; to her, most days, her family was underfoot.

He was ashamed that he had, not only yelled at, but threatened her, in front of her family. Addison, and Geno, had enjoyed it, but it had been a bitter, tasting, victory.

The memory of his harsh words was offensive to him. He shook his head. He couldn't believe he'd threatened to render her mute. He loved the sound of her voice, even when she yelled at him. He loved everything about her.

But they were all yelling, and screaming, and pointing their fingers; he couldn't get a word in, edgewise. He'd gotten frustrated and just lost it. God, he hoped she realized that he'd never take her for granted.

He thought about Chaz and Hope. They complemented each other. Chaz wasn't dependent like Ram. He was *attentive*. He'd promised Hope that he would always put her needs above all else and he hadn't let her down, not once. Chaz liked hanging out with the guys, but not at the expense of missing a, single, moment, with his family. Hope never yelled at Chaz and he never got frustrated with her. Brock envied their relationship.

He, finally, pushed away from the door and went to take his shower.

~

Brock may not have been listening to Jodi's thoughts, but she was, sure, listening to his. And although she hadn't acknowledged his presence, she'd heard every word.

She needed to stop using hormones as an excuse for her behavior. Not only had she pushed him too far, she'd allowed her family to do likewise. She should have never let her family yell at him like that. But, not only had she let them disrespect him, she'd led the charge.

The memory of her mother pointing her finger in Brock's face made Jodi cringe. They, all, owed him an apology! Brock hadn't bullied her. They'd all bullied him!

Brock would *never* allow anyone, not even her mother, to talk to her the way she'd allowed her family to talk him. The shame was not his...It was hers.

She had let her mother give Brock hell, for a week, because he wouldn't force Ali to bring Destiny home. Jodi was ashamed of herself, because she should have put her foot down, then.

When her mother started yelling and, accusing Ali of being responsible for Destiny, almost, getting blown up, Destiny stood up and told SnowAnna to backup off him. She'd even stepped in front of Lara and dared her to mess with him. She'd stood up for her man.

Jodi thought about how JR, and her uncle, had ranted about Brock not protecting Batman. She hadn't said a word, in his defense, then either. What was wrong with her? She hadn't stood up to Ted all the years he'd abused her. And now she hadn't been woman enough to stand up for Brock.

Her eyes watered. She was letting her family mistreat her husband. No, she was helping them mistreat him! There were too many people in this house, not to have rules. And the one rule she should have insisted on was no one was to ever get out of line with her husband!

Her tears started running. She hadn't, even, acknowledged that he'd just returned home from his secret mission. He'd been out fighting demons, while they were safe in the home, he'd provided. Instead of bitching, she should have wrapped her arms around him and welcomed him home. She should have thanked *God*, he was home, safe.

She was crying, in earnest, now. No wonder Brock lost it. First she'd chosen Aurellia over him and now her family. After everything he'd done for her, she continued to put his last. She didn't mean to, but she just kept on hurting him. She started sobbing.

~

When Brock stepped out of the shower he heard Jodi crying. God, he could take anything, but that. He didn't even try to dry himself off. He needed to make this right.

He sat on the bed and pulled her in his arms. He started rocking her. "I'm sorry, Jodi. I'll never do that to you, again."

She started sobbing louder. He was apologizing to her! *"It me Broc! My ault"* Even in her mind, she was sobbing and having a hard time speaking clearly.

Brock was devastated over how hard she was crying. *"Shh. I'm sorry, Jodi. Don't cry."* He kissed her forehead and kept rocking her. One of these days he was going to get it right. He hoped she'd be patient with him, until he learned how to treat her.

The more Brock thought it was his fault, the harder she cried. She stopped trying to talk and wrapped her arm around his neck.

~

It took about thirty minutes for Jodi to compose herself. But she still didn't try to speak out loud, for fear she'd start crying again. *"I'm sorry, Brock."*

Brock looked down at her, confused. *"For what, Dimples?"*

"For treating you so disrespectfully; and allowing my family to treat you just as bad.

He lifted her off his chest and looked in her eyes. Had she lost her mind? *"What are you talking about, Dimples?"*

"I shouldn't have attacked you about that room, and I shouldn't have allowed my family to,

either. We were being so mean to you." She pouted her lips and started crying, all over again.

Brock didn't know what to say, so he just pulled her back up against his chest. They *had* been out of control, that's why he'd lost it.

But their behavior was no excuse, for his. He'd threatened them with his powers and he was ashamed of himself. The great "Seraphiel" had stooped low enough to bullying women. He'd let those women raise their hands, for permission to speak, like they were children. Shame on him.

It was a relief that she wasn't crying because he'd been cruel to her. They'd both made mistakes tonight and he would make it up to her. "I'm sorry, Jodi. I wish I could take my words back, but I can't. It breaks my heart that anything could make me be cruel to you."

"I let my mother point her finger in your face, Brock. That was enough to send anybody over the edge."

He laughed. "You know Cutie doesn't think of me as her son-in-law. That, little, lady thinks I'm her son."

That was the truth. Her mother always

reminded her that Wolf was *her* son. Lara and Amanda called him their big brother. Hezekiah, really, believed he'd planted the seed that created Brock. But she still was going to get it straight with them, and everyone else, not to treat him that way, again. "Let's take our children and run away, for a while."

He laughed again. "Run away from home?" But he liked that idea. They could take a couple of days away from the crowd. "Where do you want to go, Baby?"

"I'd say my house, but Arak is staying there." She smiled.

"We can kick his butt out, for a few days!"

She rose up and put her arms around his neck. "Let's go in the morning, then." She wanted to forget everything that had happened. Her family could have the room and whole damn estate for the next two or three days. She kissed him. *"I love you, Brock."*

Brock groaned and kissed her back. He lifted her and straddled her on his lap. It didn't take much to get him in the mood for his woman. He reached down and pulled her gown over her head.

It had been over a year, they had two babies and another on the way, but the sight of her, naked, body still gave him a thrill. It always would. *"I need you, Dimples."*

Jodi leaned her head back, and trembled, as Brock caressed her breast. She pushed him back, flat, on the bed. *"I love you, Boo."*

~

They'd always had a healthy sex life, but Jodi had just taken it up a notch. His woman had dropped a load of TNT on him, and Brock couldn't move! He could barely breathe! If he didn't know better, he'd swear he was paralyzed; except his insides were still tingling. *"Damn Jodi!"* He tried to reach for her, but could only move his fingers! He was tapping them on the mattress, like Morse code.

Jodi was as out of breath as he was, but she laughed at him. *"What's the matter, Boo."*

He tried again, but his arms were like lead. He kept tapping him fingers. *"Come here, woman."*

Jodi, crawled and, straddled his waist. She looked down on him, with her elbows propped on his chest. She tried to keep from laughing, but Boo looked like he'd been rung out to dry. *"You rang?"* she teased. She leaned down, blew on and then, kissed his, soaked, chest.

Finally able to move his weak arms, he ran his fingers through her, soaked, hair. *"Five thousand years was too long to wait, before I found you. Each day was worse, and longer, than the one before. Now that I've found you, five thousand years won't be enough time to share with you, Dimples."*

That was the sad, truth. They'd always want one more day. She laid her head on this chest. *"I know, Boo."*

He stroked his fingers up and down her back. He didn't know how long it would be before that great judgment day…it could be tomorrow. He'd wasted too much time. He thought about Chaz and Ali. Those boys were teaching him how to treat a woman. *"I'm not going to hang out in the den, as much, Dimples. You and I are going to start spending more quality time together; away from the estate."*

"I'd like that. Destiny told us about Ali

taking her to Italy. I was envious," she admitted. 'But I know you can't leave; you have a lot of men under your command. I understand that, Boo."

"That won't matter, Dimples. I can monitor the situation from anywhere in the world." He didn't know why he hadn't thought of it in the first place. "Where would you like to go, first?"

"India. I've always wanted to see the Taj Mahal."

"Then India, it is."

"What about the construction?"

"Ditto, H and Lorraine are in control of that. Ram can handle the team for a night or two, whenever we leave." Then he laughed. "Cutie can run the estate. She already thinks she's the woman of the house." He knew that was a sore spot for Jodi.

She groaned and hit his chest. "Don't ruin a perfect moment, Brock. How did you know they were too much for me?"

"I know my wife. I make jokes, but that's why I told Ditto to build H's house first. It doesn't bother me, because I never had a mother, but I knew it was not good for mothers and daughters to *live under one roof."*

"What bothers me the most, is she, and Sarah, don't even knock on the door when they come to get the girls. They barge in like it's their right."

He hadn't realized that. *"Why don't you say something, Dimples?"*

"I'm a coward. Don't you know that by now?"

He laughed. *"Yeah, baby, I know. I'll talk to H about it. As a matter of fact, we need to have a meeting to establish some house rules. Don't you think?"*

"The first one will be nobody disrespects my husband!"

Since the original attack on the estate, by the humans, and then the demon attack; he and his team had stepped back from their nightly duties. They knew another attack, on the estate, could, and probably would, happen. Arak was making plans for the tri state attack on the demons. Chaz had situated the field guards so they were now covering the park, as well.

He'd done all he could for her family. The majority of them were secure behind the estate's gates. The others would be there before long. It was time to focus on his wife, and children.

They started talking about all the places she wanted to see; and places he wanted to show her. From this day forward, theirs would be a life of adventure.

They both dozed off.

CHAPTER 23

Floyd was in his office talking with Sal. Michael had requested they spend time together. "I know that you've always wanted to be a priest, but in this house, we are more non-denominational."

"I believe we each serve in our own way. I am Catholic and hold those traditions dear to my heart. But more than dogma, I just want to serve," Sal responded.

Floyd knew Sal had lost everything, when he walked away from his life. He ventured that there were probably some personal things, like family photos, that could never be replaced. Floyd and no one else would go to his house and remove anything, because then it would be suspect. His, so called, friends had probably confiscated everything, anyway. But there were two things Floyd could give him that were just as worthy, new or used. He reached in his drawer and pulled them out. "I got these for you."

Sal smiled and reached for the Catholic Bible

and rosary. He held them up to his heart. "Thank you, Floyd." He couldn't believe how good these people were to him. Especially considering how they'd become acquainted, in the first place. Even the women, last night, had included him in their rant. Strange as it were, he got a kick out of it. It made him feel like he was a part of the family. Although his poor son, Geno, should learn to keep his mouth shut. He'd been embarrassed when the boy called the women 'hens'.

Floyd and Sal, both, heard a baritone voice shout out, "Preacha!"

Floyd's heart leaped, in conjunction with his legs. The smile on his face was wide enough to see his wisdom teeth. He walked, with excitement, out the door.

~

Smittie walked towards him, flanked by his other four brothers. "What cha know about Jesus, Preacha?" he questioned.

"He's *alright*!" Floyd walked into his arms. He felt like a little kid. His heart was bubbling over. He missed *his* big brother. They talked every day, but it was nothing like being in his presence.

He loved all his brothers and they were all close, but Smittie was like a father to him. No matter what life threw at him, he got through it largely, because of Smittie.

When they were growing up, the three older ones took care of the three younger ones. Hezekiah's boy was Luther. Elijah's was Howard's. He was Smittie's.

Smittie palmed his cheek and kissed the other. "You look good, Baby Boy."

His four brothers stood back and watched them. The look on Floyd's face was one of rapture, like he'd just been rescued from them, again. "Look at him." Hezekiah smirked.

"You'd think we've been mistreating him, or something," Elijah added.

Smittie turned around and squinted. "You better not had been." He loved Floyd. From the day he was brought home from the hospital, Floyd was his baby. When they were young, he'd gotten into many fights, with those twins over the way they'd double teamed his boy. He looked back at Floyd. "Have they been treating you right?"

Floyd laughed. "Yeah, man. What are you

doing here?" He finally asked.

"I had to bring Faith, because her car is down. I heard the women were going to kill you men, if she didn't get here today." He laughed.

"Man, those women..." He stopped and looked around. "Where are they?" he whispered to his other brothers.

Hezekiah laughed. "They're upstairs."

"Man those women went crazy last night. They ran Brock out of his, own, home." He laughed. "Come on in the office and have a seat."

~

Floyd introduced Smittie to Sal. Sal saw the effect Smittie's presence had on Floyd. He was jubilant. "It's good to meet you, Smittie."

"Same here." Smittie smiled, shaking Sal's hand. Then he turned back to his brothers. "This is a nice place you guys got here."

"I'd offer to take you on a tour, but, SnowAnna and I have a meeting this morning with Lightwings, and his grandchildren. Besides, I'm sure you'll enjoy it more with your boy, anyway," Hezekiah said. "Make sure you take him to the 'wolf' den, Floyd."

"Lightwings is here?" Smittie's eyes lit up. He'd always liked that old Indian. He was a good man.

"Yeah," Hezekiah said soulfully. "You guys fill him in," he instructed his brothers and walked out the door.

Floyd's smile vanished. He nodded his head.

"What's going on, Preacha?" Smittie knew his boy. In the blink of an eye, Floyd's whole mood changed.

"Let me get you guys some coffee first." He stood up and turned his back to Smittie. It was heartbreaking what SnowAnna's brother had done to his family. Smittie would, no doubt, take it as hard and they had.

~

Hezekiah and SnowAnna walked into Ali's suite of rooms. Lara, James and Nantan were already there. Nantan, again, looked to be in shock. His eyes were red, from crying. But then so was everyone else's. "What happened?" Hezekiah asked, looking to Ali for answers.

Before Ali could say anything, Hania walked in the room and closed the door behind him. He'd seen it all, so he knew what was about to happen. "Have a seat, both of you," he said to Snow and Hezekiah.

~

Once everyone was seated Hania took control of the meeting. Ali was, more than, grateful, because he didn't think Destiny could recite it one more time. It had been heart wrenching last night and even more so this morning, when they'd told Nantan. When Lara and James made their way in, Lara took one look at Destiny and started to cry. She knew they knew. The three were hugging each other and crying like little scared kids. They *had* been three innocent, little, children drawn into this corrupt world of the occult. Neither of them wanted Amanda, Jodi or Kwanita, to be burdened with this story; they had not been invited to the meeting. Brock had not been informed, either. He, Jodi and their children had left this morning for some, long overdue, quiet time.

~

Hania started to speak. "My son was a weak man. When he met his wife, I knew she was evil. I begged him not to marry her." He frowned at the memory of that conversation. "I told him their union would bring nothing but trouble to his life…and this family. He had the gift of second sight and I pleaded with him to take a look to see for himself, what I'd seen. But he refused. He said he didn't want to see anything that would keep him from the woman he loved."

He paused for a moment and looked across the room. "He married her and moved to another reservation, a hundred miles away. They were fine, at first. They came to visit me, to bring Seke when was she was first born. She was a beautiful baby and I loved her. We'd travel back and forth visiting each other. I thought maybe my vision had been wrong, because the child was happy and her parents loved her. Then we had a fight, and stopped speaking for two years. I now know that fight was orchestrated to get me out of their lives."

"Why?" SnowAnna asked. She remembered when it happened.

Hania looked at Lara. "Your daughter was nine years old the last time she came to visit them. That's when they moved back to my reservation. The minute she got there she told me she wanted to go home. I knew something was wrong, but she wouldn't tell me, so I brought her home."

"Yes and she never told us why. She just said she was ready to come home." Hezekiah looked at Lara. He had a feeling he was not going to like what he was about to hear. If that bastard raped his child, Brock was going to have to bring his back! He sat up straight in his chair. "What happened to my daughter in Montana, Lightwings?"

SnowAnna's hands starting trembling. She looked at Lara. "What did my brother do to you, Baby?"

Lara couldn't answer. She covered her eyes and started crying. James pulled her into his arms. She'd cried herself to sleep last night, when she realized where he'd been and why. His eyes were red, too.

Destiny and Nantan were, also, crying. This was a hot mess.

~

Hania started talking, again. "After I brought her home, I had a vision to see what had upset the child."

"Tell me, Father?" SnowAnna asked, scared

to know the answer.

Hania took a deep breath and started talking again. No one said a word as he took them on a, detailed, trip into the past.

SnowAnna had her hand over her mouth, trying to keep from screaming. But she wasn't doing a very good job of it. "Oh God!" she cried out. In her mind she could see her child, running in those woods, trying to hide from those monsters. She could feel how terrified her baby was. She wanted to pick her up, in her arms and protect her. She was trying to get a vision, like she'd done with Hania. She wanted to go back in time and change this. She stood and started hyperventilating. "Why can't I see it? I need to go *save* my baby?" she cried out.

Hania grabbed her. "No! You can't, Snow. You'll change too many lives, including Destiny's and Ali's. Don't you think I thought about it?" Hania warned.

Hezekiah wasn't any help to her. He was holding his head in the palm of his, trembling hand. He'd willfully driven his daughter into the arms of danger. Had gotten out of his car and handed his baby over to a, damn, serial killer! He moaned.

Lara, Nantan and Destiny were crying, again. James and Ali felt helpless. This tragedy was one that would tear normal families apart.

Hania finished telling them all he had seen, from Lara and Seke playing hide and seek, to how Destiny found out. By the time he was finished, he was crying, too. "I warned my son not to marry that evil, despicable, woman."

~

H looked up. His eyes were full of hate and rage. "You warned your son! Your son! What about me! Why didn't you warn me, Lightwings! You saw what they would do and you still let me give my child to your, psychopathic, son!"

"No. I didn't see that, Hezekiah. If I had I would have stopped him from killing both these children's mothers."

"Then what did you see, Father!" SnowAnna shouted. She was taking Hezekiah's side on this. "What the hell did you see?"

"I saw that she grew up in evil occult practices. I knew that she would persuade him to join that occult. I knew he would forsake all that his mother, and I instilled in our children. I knew he would give up his faith in God. But I *never* saw them hurt these children!" He shook his head. "I never saw that!"

~

Hezekiah looked at Lara. He was brokenhearted. "Why didn't you tell me, daughter?" Didn't you trust me?" His voice cracked. "Didn't you know your daddy would have killed that bastard?" His face contorted. "I would have never let him get away with traumatizing my child. I would have killed them both. Your mama and I would have raised Seke, Nantan and Destiny. Didn't you know that, Lara?" He put his face in his hands. "We would have kept all of you children safe." This was killing Hezekiah.

From the time he was a teenager, he'd prided himself in protecting his family. He'd killed anybody, who put his family in danger; and never once went to jail. The neighbors all knew what he and his twin did, but no one ever came forward. Not because they were afraid of them, but because they kept the hood safe, from the *real* criminals.

He and E had earned a reputation and became known as, *'The Legendary Walker twins! A law unto themselves!"* They never went looking for trouble, but, always, met it head on. None of the kids in their neighborhood got involved in gangs, for fear of coming up against him and E.

But this time he hadn't protected his child. This time, he'd been the one to put his daughter in the path of danger. No, not path, arms! It was no wonder she didn't trust him to keep her safe. He felt like a fraud. He looked over at Lara. His breathing was labored. "Didn't you know that, child?"

Hezekiah's blood pressure accelerated and his heart raced; both beyond control. Then a sharp pain pierced his brain. He knew he was having a heart attack and stroke. Snow was right, he was an old coot. He needed to tell her he was sorry for putting their daughter in harm's way...before it was too late. "Aw sah ee, sssnoo." He fell, forward, to the floor.

SnowAnna screamed. "HEZEKIAH!" She knelt down beside him and screamed, "Wolf!"

Lara, James and Destiny, jumped up and ran

over to him, "Daddy!"

Nantan fell, at his side, next to Snow. "Dad!" His baritone voice sounded like a little boy.

Even, Ali panicked. This wasn't another anxiety attack. This was a stroke and heart attack, combined! He couldn't get control of Hezekiah's vitals! He wouldn't die, but he could become incapacitated! *"Brock! Help!"*

Hania was the only one who remained, calmly, seated. Life had to have her way.

~

Brock appeared in the room, alone. "Damn it, Ali. We agreed!" he yelled and knelt down beside SnowAnna and Nantan. He grabbed Hezekiah's hand. His face had already twisted, to one side. "Come on, Old Man. Don't do this!" He calmed his pulse and heart rate. But he was too late, the damage was done. H had had, both, a heart attack and a massive stroke.

~

SnowAnna stood up and closed her eyes. Her brother had destroyed his family; she'd be damned if he was going to destroy hers! With tears streaking down her face, she whispered, "Forgive me!"

~

SnowAnna walked into Ali's suite of rooms. Lara, James and Nantan were already there. Hania walked in, right behind her, and closed the door. "Have a seat," he told her.

"Where's Hezekiah?" Ali asked.

"He's in Floyd's office. Smittie arrived this morning and I told him to spend this time with his brothers," SnowAnna answered, as she sat down.

"He really needs to be here, Cutie," Ali said. He didn't want Destiny to have to tell this tragic story, again.

She squinted. "My husband must *never* know what we are about to discuss..." She stared at each of them. "...Or that this meeting *ever* took place."

Hania looked at his daughter, and nodded.

A chill ran down Ali's spine...

~

...Déjà vu.

EPILOGUE

"I'd offer to take you on a tour, but SnowAnna and I have a meeting this morning with Lightwings, and his grandchildren. Besides, I'm sure you'll enjoy it more with your boy, anyway," Hezekiah said. "Make sure you take him to the 'wolf' den, Floyd."

"Lightwings is here?" Smittie's eyes lit up. He'd always liked that old Indian. He was a good man.

"Yeah," Hezekiah said, soulfully. "You guys fill him in," he instructed his brothers and walked out the door.

He wished he could stay and visit with Smittie. It had been a long time since he'd seen him. Plus, anything was better than this upcoming meeting. He was certain it had more to do with Destiny's and Nantan's parents. Those two were the vilest *humans* he'd come across, ever. Hatred may have taken them over, last night; but Hatred hadn't made him beat Nantan, fifteen years ago.

If Nantan had been his son, he would have been proud, no matter what his choice in life. Hell, he was proud of him now.

Nantan and all the young men had told him that Nantan was a computer geek. That he'd made his living designing video games. He donated part of his salary back to the manufacturer, so the children's wards at all the hospitals, could get the games, for free.

Nantan had also developed games for special needs children; to help them learn. He'd even figured out a way to make games for old folks, to help them stay agile. He'd promised once he got his laptop he'd set it up in the 'wolf den' for his old man.

Hezekiah never played one, personally, but he watched the news; those games were the hottest things going. When he'd told Nantan how proud he was of him, the man's eyes lit up. Hezekiah understood that. Every man wanted his father to be proud of him. Yeah, Nantan was a decent young man; and he was his son now.

~

When Hezekiah reached the end of the hall, SnowAnna was waiting on him. "Am I late?" he asked.

"No. They decided it was too soon to talk about it. Plus, I told them Smittie was here and you wanted to spend some time with him."

"I wonder what they wanted to talk about," Hezekiah said.

"It doesn't matter. Go back in with your brothers. Enjoy them, you old coot."

"Alright." Hezekiah smiled and turned to walk away.

SnowAnna stopped him and wrapped her arms around him. "I love you, Hezekiah. I always have."

Hezekiah hugged her. "I know that, Wife. I love you, too."

She didn't let go; instead, she, desperately, squeezed him tighter. She'd just risked everything for him.

The minute he fell to the floor, she'd known how bad it was. She'd felt his spirit ebbing away from her. Wolf had been able to stop it, but the damage was already done to his body. She couldn't take the risk that he may, eventually, recover and she wasn't about to let him become a vegetable. Brock taking him to Paradise today, or any other day, was out of the question.

She didn't know if she'd angered mother time and, in that moment, she hadn't cared. She'd done what she had to do, because she wasn't going to lose her husband.

She hadn't known if she could do it, but it had been worth, everything, to try. She'd simply stood up and whispered, 'forgive me'. Then she envisioned the time, and space, where she needed to be. When she opened her eyes she found herself standing in her suite of rooms. She'd look at her watch and realized she'd jumped, backwards in time by one hour.

She'd run down the stairs, as fast as she could, to stop Hezekiah from going into that room. To keep him from hearing those horrific details of what happened to their daughter. To keep him from hearing what *her* brother had done. She'd run as fast as she could to keep the love of her life from imploding.

Her brother had destroyed his family; she'd be damned if she was going to let him destroy hers. Nantan and Destiny were her children, now. She'd make up to them, their children, and their children's children, what her brother had done to their mothers. She'd make it up to Lara for trusting her into the care of that psychopath. She would gladly do that! But she would *not* lose Hezekiah!

It was perfect timing that Smittie had showed up today. When Hezekiah got with his brothers he could be, happily, occupied for hours. It was a good sign that fate, just, might be on her side. She could only hope and pray.

~

Hezekiah felt SnowAnna trembling. He pulled away and lifted her chin. "What's the matter, Wife?"

She was on the verge of crying. "I'm sorry I was mad at you about that, old silly, room." Her eyes watered. "You mean more to me than a room, Hezekiah. You mean more to me than anything…or anybody. I hope you know that."

He wiped her eyes. "I know that, Snow. I'm

just glad you let me sleep in my bed, last night."

She hugged him again, even tighter. "Me too. I don't ever want to sleep in a bed, or wake up in one, without you next to me." Then she released him. "Now go on, you old coot. Your brothers are waiting."

He kissed her cheek. "See you later, alright? Maybe we can have a date in the theatre, just the two of us. We can watch one of those sappy movies you like."

"No. We will watch what you like. Maybe "Shaft" or "The Negotiator"." Her husband loved Samuel L. Jackson.

Hezekiah frowned, "Now I know something's wrong. You hate those types of movies."

"But I love you. No go on, your brothers are waiting." She pushed him away from her.

~

Hezekiah walked back down the hall. This was great. He could spend time with Smittie and the boys. When he got to the doorway, he felt the hair on the back of his neck stand up. He had an uneasy feeling, like he was being watched. He turned around to see SnowAnna, still standing in the same spot. Staring at him. Something *was* wrong. "Snow?"

She smiled, waved and walked away.

NEXT:

Arakiel's
FAITH
(A Spirit Mate Love Story)
(Book 7)

A PARANORMAL LOVE STORY

Made in the USA
Las Vegas, NV
13 January 2021

15833362R00203